Dear Maudie,

I never thought I'd be doing this, but under the circumstances, you are the only person who can help me. I've never gotten over a crush I had on a woman in college. I've tried to get the lady out of my mind, but nothing has worked. She was recently divorced, and I'm wondering whether I should contact her. Am I foolish to think she might learn to care for me?

Torch Carrier

Emmy Bakersfield, aka "Maudie," read the letter and decided that somewhere out there was a very lucky woman. Torch Carrier sounded like just the kind of man any woman could love.

ELAINE CAMP

has known since the age of ten that she wanted to be a writer. Now she is both a reporter and an accomplished novelist. Her training as a journalist comes in handy when she travels, helping her to notice the details that later turn up in her books.

Dear Reader:

SILHOUETTE DESIRE is an exciting new line of contemporary romances from Silhouette Books. During the past year, many Silhouette readers have written in telling us what other types of stories they'd like to read from Silhouette, and we've kept these comments and suggestions in mind in developing SILHOUETTE DESIRE.

DESIREs feature all of the elements you like to see in a romance, plus a more sensual, provocative story. So if you want to experience all the excitement, passion and joy of falling in love, then SILHOUETTE DESIRE is for you.

Karen Solem
Editor-in-Chief
Silhouette Books

ELAINE CAMP
Love Letters

Silhouette Desire

Published by Silhouette Books New York

America's Publisher of Contemporary Romance

Silhouette Books by Elaine Camp

To Have, to Hold (ROM #99)
Devil's Bargain (ROM #173)
For Love or Money (SE #113)
This Tender Truce (ROM #270)
Love Letters (DES #207)

SILHOUETTE BOOKS
300 E. 42nd St., New York, N.Y. 10017

Copyright © 1985 by Deborah E. Camp

Distributed by Pocket Books

ISBN: 0-373-05207-3

First Silhouette Books printing May, 1985

10 9 8 7 6 5 4 3 2

America's Publisher of Contemporary Romance

Printed in the U.S.A.

To Bob Kelley,
for showing a girl
a good time.

Love
Letters

1

Dear Maudie,

I never thought I'd be doing this, but under the circumstances, I have come to the conclusion that you are the only person who can help me with my problem.

I'm a thirty-year-old man who has never gotten over a crush I had on a woman during my college years. Believe me, I've tried to get this lady out of my mind, but nothing has worked. The lady—let's call her Susie for our purposes here—was recently divorced, and I'm wondering whether or not I should contact her. Am I foolish to think that she might learn to care for me the way I care for her?

Sign me,
Torch Carrier

Dear T.C.,

Of course you should contact her! Don't come on like a bulldozer—it takes time to get past a divorce—but Susie could probably use a friend now. Be advised, however, that Susie will have changed from college days, and she might not be the woman you remember. Good luck.

Maudie

Maude Edith Bakersfield removed her reading glasses and rubbed her weary eyes with her thumb and forefinger; then she folded the morning edition of the Atlanta newspaper and laid it to one side. Her vision blurred for a few seconds before her blue eyes focused on the small hills of letters on her desk. Across the room Bertha Glasser ripped open another envelope, read the letter inside and placed it on one of the paper hills covering her own desk.

Bertha glanced up and smiled. "Taking a break, Emmy?"

"My eyes are about to fall out of their sockets." Emmy turned to face her word processor, then pressed a couple of keys. The machine began printing out the advice column she had just finished. "Today's column was interesting. I especially liked the letter from that guy who still has a thing for a woman he knew in college." She glanced at the stacks of mail again and frowned. "We're certainly getting a lot of depressing letters in lately."

"It's this lousy weather," Bertha said, glancing behind Emmy at the floor-to-ceiling windows that afforded a view of the overcast Atlanta skyline. "It seems as if it's been raining steadily for weeks!" She returned her attention to the letters on her desk. "Marriages on the skids are heading the list this month."

"Have you found any unusual ones?" Emmy asked, coming around the desk to peer over her assistant's shoulder.

"Not really . . . wait a minute." Bertha read over the letter before her and laughed. "Here's a winner! This lady says her husband wants to make love to her at least six times a week and that her mother thinks his sexual appetite is perverted. She wants to know if she should take her mother's advice and talk to her husband about his abnormal behavior."

Emmy laughed and held out her hand. "Give me. I'll put that one in one of the columns next week."

"What advice are you going to give her?" Bertha asked, handing the letter over to Emmy.

Emmy went back to her own desk, sat down and thought a few moments before answering. "My advice is to make love, not war." She typed in the letter, answered it and glanced at the others waiting for her attention. "I'm going to put in a month's worth of columns now, just in case I get bogged down while I'm on my publicity tour."

"How's that progressing?" Bertha looked at the framed dust cover on the wall near Emmy's desk. "*The Best of 'Ask Maudie,'*" Bertha read aloud. "I can't believe that it will be coming out next month."

A satisfied smile settled on Emmy's lips. "I know what you mean. I'm meeting a couple of public relations representatives for cocktails this evening to discuss the promotional tour." Her heart fluttered with a bout of nerves. "I hope I can handle all this publicity stuff. How did all of this happen, Bertha?" Emmy implored her assistant. "A few years ago no one had even heard of

Maudie. I had trouble just getting someone to syndicate the column!"

"You deserve all the best," Bertha said with a warm smile. "You've had a rocky road to travel lately, and it's about time good things started happening to you."

"Thanks." Emmy returned the woman's kind smile. "Speaking of good things, I think I've got a buyer for my house."

"Great! I know you'll be glad to dump that burden."

"And how," Emmy agreed. "That house is my last link with Jerry. Once it's sold, I'll be free to start all over again."

"How do you like living in an apartment?"

"I like it fine. Anything's better than rambling around that house and bumping into memories at every turn."

The telephone buzzed and Bertha answered it. She sent a comical look across the room to Emmy as she put the caller on hold.

"Speak of the devil . . . your ex-husband is on the line and he'd like to talk to you."

Emmy took a deep breath, then exhaled before she picked up the receiver. "Hello, Jerry. What can I do for you?" she asked in an impersonal tone.

"Plenty," Jerry snapped. "I hear that you've got the house up for sale."

"That's right, and I've even got some buyers on the hook."

"You can't sell it."

Emmy bristled. "Oh, no? You just watch me. What do you expect me to do with it? Declare it a national monument and hang a sign outside that says 'Jerry Jennings Slept Here'? We could place quite a few of those signs around Atlanta, couldn't we?" She smiled across at Bertha, who stuck an imaginary knife into the air and twisted it.

"You can cut the sarcasm, Emmy," Jerry growled. "You can't sell it until my appeal is acted on."

"Your appeal?"

"Yes, I've petitioned the court for half of what you get from the sale of the house, and a judge has to decide whether or not to hear the appeal. Until that time, you can't sell the house. Ask your lawyer. He'll tell you all about it."

Emmy's blue eyes narrowed to slits, and her voice dropped to a dangerous purr. "Why don't you let go of me, Jerry? We're divorced. Why don't you just get out of my life?"

"I want what is rightfully mine!"

Emmy counted to ten, but it didn't do any good. She could feel her blood beginning to boil. "I'm not going to argue this point again."

"I've got something else to tell you—"

"I've got something to tell you, too, Jerry. Are you listening?"

"Yes, what is it?"

Emmy waited a moment, then slammed down the receiver, making Bertha break into raucous laughter. Emmy glared at the instrument as if it embodied her ex-husband. "He is the most spiteful, spoiled, insensitive—"

"What's he up to now?" Bertha cut in, her brown eyes alight with interest.

"He's petitioned the court for half of what I get on the house," Emmy explained. "Until the judge clears this up, I can't sell. Can you believe that?"

"He's like a dog with a bone. He just won't give it up."

Emmy grinned at Bertha's comparison. "He's being a

pain in the neck, that's for sure. For a man who was hot for a divorce, he sure is hard to shake."

"He's changed his mind, I guess. Maybe he's beginning to realize what he lost." Bertha tore open another envelope and shrugged her rounded shoulders.

"He's the one who went to graze on greener pastures," Emmy pointed out. "When I finally break all ties with Jerry, I swear I'll never get tangled up with another man."

"Uh-uh-uh!" Bertha wagged a finger at her. "Don't make such hasty vows, honey. I felt the same way when I divorced my first husband, but then Arnie came along and all those promises I made went right up in smoke." Her ruddy face crinkled into a grin. "Thank heavens! Arnie's the best thing that ever happened to me."

"I don't know. . . ." Emmy said doubtfully as she gathered a few things from her desk and placed them in her briefcase. "I'm going home, Bertha. I'll work on these other columns tonight after that cocktail meeting."

"Okay. Don't burn the midnight oil too late. See you in the morning."

"Right." She slipped into her raincoat, grabbed her briefcase, purse and umbrella and left the office.

The rain had let up as Emmy stepped outside and headed on foot for her apartment building, located only a few blocks from the office. She glanced up at the cloud banks and sighed. Would it ever stop raining? she wondered as she quickened her strides and hoped she'd make it home before the skies opened up again.

The weather matched her mood as her thoughts circled around Jerry and his court appeal. It would be a load off her mind to sell the house, not to mention the financial burden that would be lifted. Jerry was such a leech! What gave him the idea that he deserved any of the money she would get from the house? She'd made all the mortgage payments. If she had depended on Jerry to make them, the mortgage company would have foreclosed years ago.

Emmy reached her apartment building just as another sheet of rain fell on the city. She ducked inside, greeted the doorman and took the stairs to the second floor.

Inside her apartment she went to her study and set her briefcase on her cherry-wood desk. After shrugging out of her raincoat and kicking off her heels, she dropped into a comfortable chair and stared out the window at the bleak weather.

Looking around the tastefully decorated room, Emmy smiled with satisfaction. She liked the apartment, and she didn't mind living alone. Oh, there were times when she wished for companionship—someone to greet her at the door with a warm kiss—but, all in all, she didn't regret being single. She'd been alone so often during the last year of her marriage to Jerry that it had given her time to adjust to being by herself and on her own. The only thing she really missed was someone to talk with in the evenings over dinner. The television had become her dinner partner, but it was a poor substitute for the stimulation of another human being.

Bertha was right, she mused as she began unpinning her thick, black hair from its French braid and letting it fall to her shoulders. It was time for her luck to change. Looking back over the past few years, it seemed that her life had progressed at breakneck speed, giving her little time to digest all the things that had happened.

It seemed ages ago, instead of just seven years, that she had married Jerry the summer after she had graduated from college. Jerry had proved to be an erratic provider, moving from one job to another, and Emmy had been the steady wage earner. She'd worked as a reporter for a weekly newspaper outside Atlanta, and that was where "Ask Maudie" had begun. The publisher had mentioned that he'd like to run a regular advice column, and Emmy had volunteered. Her degree in sociology had helped her examine problems and suggest solutions, and the column had become the most well read part of the newspaper.

She'd added a different twist by encouraging follow-up correspondence so that her readers would know whether or not her advice had worked. It wasn't unusual for Maudie to correspond with someone over a span of several months until the problem was resolved. She'd approached a few syndicates about her column, but was unsuccessful in her attempt to reach a wider audience until a noted syndicated columnist wrote about "Ask Maudie." This led to a series of interviews for national magazines and, lo and behold, a major syndicate approached her and offered to publish her advice column.

ACTION Syndicates signed her up and, within two years "Ask Maudie" was appearing in more than fifty newspapers across the country.

Jerry quit his work as a writer for a petroleum magazine and announced that he was going to manage Emmy's business. Sensing that he was looking for an excuse to be his own boss since he had trouble working for anyone else, Emmy consented to Jerry's idea, though his vision of managing her business consisted of playing golf every day and poker with "the boys" every evening.

Emmy stood up and wandered to the stereo, switched it on and closed her eyes as soft classical music washed over her, soothing the savage beast within. The demise of a marriage, no matter how hollow the relationship might have become, was a horrendous ordeal. Even though her love for Jerry had died long before she'd sued for divorce, the pain still lingered when she thought of those months of meetings with lawyers, judges and all the other strangers who had opened up her private life and examined it. The most painful thing of all had been Jerry's admission in court that he had found someone else because Emmy had been so wrapped up in her career that he seldom saw her. He had followed that up with some legal hocus-pocus about how he had managed Emmy's career and, therefore, had a stake in it.

The judge had believed him and rewarded him with a lucrative settlement, ordering Emmy to pay Jerry a hefty sum for "all the work he has done in guiding your career successfully."

What rubbish! Emmy seethed inwardly and switched off the stereo. And now Jerry wanted half of what she would receive from the sale of the house!

The few times Jerry *had* stuck his nose in her business, he had botched things up. When her contract with ACTION came up for renewal, Jerry had almost ruined everything by demanding an outrageous salary increase for Emmy. In the nick of time she had stepped in and compromised, thus saving her pleasant business tie with ACTION's owner, Tom Griven.

When Emmy was approached by a major publisher to compile the best of her letters and answers for a book, Jerry had nearly spoiled that deal by threatening to take the proposal to other publishing houses if the publisher didn't agree to double their advance money offer *and* give him five percent of the royalties, along with twenty percent for Emmy. Once again, Emmy had come to the rescue and accepted the publisher's gracious offer.

Emmy had presented these horror stories in court, but Jerry's lawyer had been clever. He'd argued that if

Emmy had given Jerry free rein she might be a richer woman. The judge had agreed.

Thunder rolled across the sky, breaking through Emmy's memories. She pressed the gloomy thoughts to the back of her mind and went into her bedroom to shower and dress for the cocktail meeting. Once Jerry's appeal had been addressed, she hoped it would be the end of her ties with him. Her decision to divorce Jerry Jennings had been the most difficult one she had ever made, but once she had made it she had been determined to see it through to the finish. Why wouldn't he let it end? Why was he hounding her?

Maybe he was having second thoughts about their divorce, as Bertha had suggested.

"It's too late, Jerry," Emmy said as she undressed. "You should have thought about that before you burned all your bridges behind you. There's no turning back now."

Looking crisp and smart in an off-white linen suit, black heels, onyx earrings and necklace and a black, wide-brimmed hat, Emmy was led to a table near the back of the club. A man in his thirties stood up to greet her. His blond hair was sparse, his green eyes friendly.

"Hello, Miss Bakersfield. I'm Pete Bitters."

"Hello," Emmy said, shaking his hand before sitting in the chair he indicated. "So you're Tom Griven's friend?"

"Yes, that's right. Tom and I have been friends since high school. I was so pleased when he asked my firm to represent you and your new book."

"Thank you. The feeling is mutual, and please call me Emmy."

"Emmy." He smiled as if sounding out her name. "Where did you come by that nickname?"

"My initials," she explained. "Maude Edith. M.E."

"Oh." He nodded, catching on. "That's nice."

"It's preferable to either Maude or Edith."

"I agree. You look more like an Emmy. I bet most people are surprised when they meet you. I would have thought that the woman who writes 'Ask Maudie' would be in her fifties or sixties. You must be in your twenties."

"Twenty-eight," she supplied without hesitation, "going on sixty."

Pete threw back his head and laughed, and Emmy decided she liked him. A man who laughed easily would be a pleasure to work with.

"So you're going to head up my publicity tour?" she asked, steering the conversation to the business at hand.

"Not exactly." He glanced at the waiter, then back to her. "What would you like to drink?"

"A Bloody Mary, please."

"And two more Scotch and waters here," Pete added.

Emmy noticed the other empty glass and equally empty chair. "Where's our other party?"

"He had to make a quick phone call. He'll be back in a minute." Pete cleared his throat, and his gaze moved past her shoulder. "He'll be the one who will guide you through the tour."

"I see."

"Here he comes." Pete lifted a hand and motioned toward Emmy. "Let me introduce you. . . ."

Emmy turned in her chair to face the man who was approaching the table. A shock ran through her as she took in the newcomer's devil-may-care grin and teasing brown eyes. It had been a while since she'd seen him, but resentment surged through her, and it took all the strength she had to summon a civil smile.

"Well, bless my soul," Emmy said softly as the broad-shouldered man stopped beside her chair. "If it isn't Whittier Hayes."

His smile was warm and well remembered. "Hello, Emmy. Are you surprised?"

"Flabbergasted," she admitted as the consequences of the meeting began to dawn on her. She looked back to Pete and could read in his expression that he knew of her acquaintance with his partner.

"That's right!" Pete said, snapping his fingers and trying to cover for himself. "You two know each other, don't you?"

"I should say so." Emmy turned back to Whit. "He kidnapped my ex-husband regularly for games of golf, not to mention the nights he won money off him at poker." *My* money, she tacked on mentally.

"I plead innocent to that last charge," Whit said as he folded his tall frame into the chair on Emmy's right. "I was the big loser in those poker games, and I bowed out early. They captured another sucker to take my place."

The waiter arrived with their drinks, giving Emmy a few moments to get her bearings. Whit Hayes, Jerry's old college buddy, was going to head up her publicity tour? Did Jerry have anything to do with this? She felt like the innocent victim of a conspiracy.

"So you're co-owner of Town Crier Public Relations?" Emmy asked when the waiter had left the table. "I remember Jerry saying something about you changing jobs a couple of years ago."

"That's right," Whit said after taking a drink of his Scotch. "I took the plunge and joined up with Pete to start our own PR firm. We're pleased that you hired us."

"I didn't," Emmy reminded him. "Tom Griven hired you."

"We were just getting around to discussing the tour,"

Pete said. "Emmy, let me assure you that our firm will ease the way for you. We want you to have fun and leave the logistics and all the problems to us."

Emmy looked at Whit. "You'll be traveling with me?"

Whit nodded. "I'll be right by your side all the way."

He meant it to be comforting, but Emmy felt a tingle of apprehension. Whit Hayes was Jerry's friend, not hers, and she didn't like the idea of Whit being involved in her business. It seemed that at every turn she was running into reminders of Jerry Jennings.

"Is there some problem, Emmy?" Pete asked, having noticed her slight frown.

"No," Emmy lied. "I'm just nervous about the tour. I'm not convinced that I'll be effective."

"You'll be great," Pete said. "I predict that your book will be a best seller."

"Please," Emmy pleaded, holding up her hands to stop his predictions. "Let's not count our chickens before they're hatched."

"Pete's right," Whit said. "We're going to make a great team, Emmy."

She looked at him fully, taking in his sandy blond hair and dark brown eyes. He hadn't lost that lopsided grin that had mowed down the girls at college. Her attention was drawn to the cut of his dark suit, and she couldn't help but notice that he still had the body of a collegiate quarterback. "Why did you decide to represent me, Whit? Why not Pete?"

He seemed taken aback, and the smile slipped from his lips. "Something wrong with me working with you, Emmy?"

"I'm not sure." She sipped her drink, making him wait for the rest of her answer. "Does Jerry know about this?"

"I don't know." His voice took on an uneasy edge. "I haven't spoken to Jerry in some time."

"Really?" She arched a brow and stared him down.

"Really." Whit looked across the table to Pete for help.

"I'm sure that once you start working with Whit any misgivings you might have will disappear," Pete said, coming to his partner's aid.

"We'll see." Emmy stared pointedly at the folder near Pete's elbow. "Do you have a schedule to show me? I don't mean to be rude, but I'm rushed for time. Could we get on with this, please?"

"Of course!" Pete almost upset his drink as he reached for the folder. He glanced nervously across the table at Whit, but his partner had dropped into a quiet mood and offered nothing more than an occasional grunt of agreement to certain points Pete made.

Emmy climbed into the cab and gave the driver her address. She didn't glance back at the two men she had left on the curb.

Whittier Hayes, of all people, she thought with a burst of frustration. She breathed a sigh of relief as the taxi put more space between her and the object of her troubled thoughts. With all the PR firms in Atlanta, why did Tom have to select Whit's company?

It *could* be a coincidence, she conceded, but the odds were against it. Jerry had probably put Whit up to this. It was just another way to keep himself involved in her life . . . and in her business.

Whit and Jerry had been almost inseparable in college, and they had kept up with each other after graduation. It was just too neat, too convenient, Emmy thought. Whit was Jerry's friend and, through Whit, Jerry could keep tabs on the success and sales of Emmy's book. Was he planning to appeal again and ask for half of what she made on the sales of the book?

"I won't stand for it," Emmy said, not realizing that she'd spoken aloud until she saw the cabbie's questioning gaze in the rearview mirror.

"Say what, lady?"

"Nothing." Emmy felt her face flame. "Let me out here and I'll walk the rest of the way."

"You sure? A looker like you shouldn't be—"

"Just let me out, please!" Emmy ordered, her voice rising with irritation.

"Sure thing!" He steered the car to the curb and braked. "Anything you say."

"Thank you." Emmy paid him and got out of the cab.

The rain had passed over the city, leaving it shining and clean smelling. Emmy set a brisk pace toward her apartment building, walking off her irritation and drawing soul-cleansing breaths of cool air.

Jerry Jennings had hounded her enough, she thought. Maybe Whit was innocent, but she wouldn't be able to work with him until she was sure of his motives. She was supposed to meet him for lunch tomorrow, and she'd pursue this matter without Pete as a third party in this private interrogation.

Whit had said he hadn't seen Jerry in a while, she recalled. For his sake, she hoped he was telling the truth. Town Crier wasn't the only public relations firm in Atlanta, and she wouldn't hesitate to ask Tom to secure another company if she felt that Whit Hayes had a motive besides publicizing her book.

2

Dear Maudie,

Bristling with eagerness, I contacted Susie as you suggested, and the results were less than rewarding. My self-confidence is at an all-time low.

Susie made it clear that she doesn't want anything to do with me. I think her attitude has something to do with my previous association with her ex-husband. She seems to think that I'm on his side, not hers. Should I launch a campaign to change her mind? If so, could you give me some tips on how to gain her trust?

Having seen her again, I'm even more smitten than I was before. Please answer me as soon as possible.

Torch Carrier

Whittier Hayes pushed aside a stack of envelopes on his writing desk and stood up, stretching lazily and issuing a noisy yawn. Crossing to the living room windows of his suburban home, he stared at the evening sky where only a few brave stars battled for brightness among the thick clouds.

Esmerelda weaved between his legs, and Whit leaned down to stroke the cat's mottled coat. She struck up a deep, continuous purr and turned her soulful gaze up to him.

"How's the budding family doing, Elda?" Whit dropped to his haunches and rubbed the cat's swollen stomach. "Who's responsible for this? Was it that white hobo? I'm surprised at you, Elda, falling for a hit-and-run artist like that one." Life stirred beneath his fingers, and Whit smiled. "You hussy."

Esmerelda sprang to her feet and padded regally to the kitchen for a midnight snack. Whit stood up again and faced the night, reminding himself to ask Pete to baby-sit Elda while he was out of town on Emmy's publicity tour. Elda was due to deliver any day now. With luck she'd have her family before Whit had to leave. A grin touched his lips when he imagined Pete's reaction to baby-sitting Elda and her brood. This would take some fast talking, Whit decided.

As Whit pressed his forehead against the cool window-pane, his breath fogged the glass and his thoughts moved ahead to the publicity tour with Emmy. He had been looking forward to it ever since he'd persuaded Pete to contact Tom Griven about the job, but now he had his doubts.

She doesn't care much for you, he told himself. That was obvious at the club tonight. Her blue eyes had been as cold as ice, freezing him to the bone and throwing him for a loop. What was with her? What had he ever done to deserve that deep freeze? Had Jerry been talking about him to her? It would be just like that guy to bad-mouth him behind his back. Jerry had always kept him away from Emmy. Was he still doing it?

Whit turned from the window as a restless frustration blew through him. He pulled his shirttails free from his waistband and unbuttoned his shirt. Before he could make it to his favorite chair, Esmerelda beat him to it. She gazed at him triumphantly and began cleaning her whiskers and paws. Laughing, Whit draped himself on the couch and stared up at the ornately carved blades of the ceiling fan. His thoughts revolved lazily and spirited him back to college, where he had first encountered the charms of Maude Edith Bakersfield.

They had worked on the yearbook together. Emmy had been Jerry's girl, and Whit had played the field. Everything was just fine until Whit started falling in love with Emmy; that was when everything had become complicated and hopeless.

"Unrequited love," Whit whispered with droll sarcasm. He laughed at himself, remembering how he had pined for Emmy and hoped she would come to her senses and realize that he, not Jerry, was the right man for her. But Emmy had married Jerry right after she'd graduated.

Whit and Jerry had continued the shallow friendship they'd begun in college. A thoughtful frown creased Whit's forehead as he examined the peculiar acquaintance he had with Jerry Jennings. He and Jerry had never particularly liked one another, and yet they had kept up a casual series of golf games and rounds of drinks after work. Looking back on it with newfound clarity, Whit wondered if he had unconsciously used Jerry to keep in touch with Emmy. Why else would he have exposed himself to Jerry's irritating personality?

Maybe he had felt sorry for Jerry after graduation. He'd witnessed Jerry's come down from big man on campus to just another guy trying to make a buck in the cold, cruel world. It had been a difficult transition for Jerry, and Whit wasn't sure that Jerry had ever adapted to not being the center of attention.

Whit, on the other hand, had been anxious to graduate. Seeing Emmy every day and working closely with her on the yearbook had been torture. She'd become engaged to Jerry, and Whit had died a little inside every time she had talked of her upcoming marriage. Whit and Jerry had graduated a year before Emmy. Whit had secured a public relations job before he graduated, but it was nine months after graduation before Jerry finally joined the staff of a company magazine.

It had been almost two years since Emmy's divorce, and Whit had thought that Jerry was completely out of the picture. After the cocktail meeting, however, he wondered if Jerry were still keeping Emmy from him.

She thinks of me as Jerry's friend, Whit thought with another burst of frustration, and why shouldn't she? After all, he had seen a lot of Jerry when Jerry had been married to Emmy, but since the divorce Whit had seen Jerry only once. He'd agreed to meet Jerry for a drink one afternoon and had come dangerously close to belting his old college buddy. Jerry had had a few too many drinks before Whit had arrived. The other man had announced that he was a free man. His divorce from Emmy was final, and Jerry had bragged that he had already had a replacement lined up.

"I'm so glad to be rid of Emmy," Jerry had said, his words slurring. "You can't imagine how terrible it was to be tied to a woman like that."

"I've always thought that you were lucky to have Emmy," Whit had said, unable to keep silent. "She's bright, ambitious and—"

"And so wrapped up in herself it's disgusting," Jerry had interrupted a bit too loudly. "All she thinks about is *her* job, *her* future and *her* money. What about me?" He stuck his thumb into his own chest, and his eyes watered. "Don't I deserve a break? Don't I deserve success?"

"From what I can see, no one has ever stopped you from making a success of yourself, Jerry."

"You don't understand," Jerry whined. "*I* was voted most likely to succeed in college, not Emmy!"

Whit leaned forward to press his point. "We're not in college anymore, Jerry. That was kid stuff, not a divine prophecy."

"Well, Emmy should have helped me more!" Jerry's lips twisted into a rubbery smirk. "But she just loves to see me crawl. She's a heartless bi—" Jerry cut off his sentence as Whit shot up from his chair and threw two bills on the table. "Hey! Where you going?"

"Anywhere but here. Good-bye, Jerry."

The memory soured in his soul, and Whit rose from the couch and went into the bathroom for a quick shower before bed. He finished undressing and stepped under the cold spray, closing his eyes and wishing he had socked Jerry that day. If he had, maybe Emmy would have realized that he had always been in her corner and that she had always had a special place in his heart.

He turned his back to the spray and began soaping his body. What was done was done. His task was to start with a clean slate and earn Emmy's trust again. She'd trusted him in college, and he knew that she had liked him. He had time on his side, since they had to work together over the next several weeks. It would be nice to work with Emmy again. Just like old times, except with an important twist. Emmy wasn't Jerry's girl anymore.

He'd launch his quest for her trust tomorrow when she was scheduled to meet him for lunch. Just the two of them.

The promise of tomorrow chased aside his earlier frustration, and he finished his shower quickly, dried off and fell into bed. He closed his eyes to let images of Emmy float through his mind. Good grief! He'd turned into a lovesick fool, and that wasn't like him. Over the years he had dated a number of women, and not one of them had made him feel downright giddy. But Emmy was different. She always had been.

Her appearance had changed, but her hold on him was still as fierce as it had been in college. Gone were the bell-bottomed jeans, T-shirts, braids and rimless glasses. These days she preferred tailored suits and flowing hair that curled at her shoulders. She had matured, but she hadn't lost the zesty gleam in her blue eyes, or that slightly husky voice that made people think she might be coming down with a cold or just recovering from one.

She was still his Emmy. Now all he had to do was convince her of that.

Emmy paid the taxi driver and slammed the car door with more force than was necessary. Ignoring the hard look the cabbie gave her, Emmy hurried into the restaurant. She was late, but she didn't care. What had begun as a nice day had become a nightmare.

She darted into the restroom and glared at her heightened color in the mirror over the sink. Her hands balled into tight fists as her lawyer's announcement burned in her mind. Her attorney had confirmed her worst fears. She couldn't sell the house until a judge made a decision on Jerry's stupid appeal.

It just wasn't fair! Hadn't Jerry messed up her life enough? The huge mortgage payments were breaking her back, but she had to keep making them until this appeal was settled. She hadn't wanted the house in the first place. It had been Jerry's idea. He'd been the one who had wanted a pool and a tennis court to impress his friends, even though Emmy had tried to talk him out of it, knowing that she would be the one who would have to keep up the payments. Bills and time payments worried her, but Jerry never lost a wink of sleep over them.

Mindful that she was keeping Whittier Hayes waiting, Emmy smoothed her hair and brought her temper under control. She gritted her teeth and emerged from the restroom, telling herself to get this over with. She spotted Whit and weaved through the tables toward him, managing a tight smile at his greeting.

"Sorry I'm late," she said as she took her seat across from him. "I've had a hectic day so far."

"Well, you can relax now."

Whit's smile reminded her of all the hours she'd spent with him on the college yearbook staff. He'd been fun back then and had always managed to make her laugh. She could use a good laugh right now.

"Would you like something to drink?" Whit asked, glancing from the waiter to Emmy.

"Iced tea," Emmy replied. She took the menu from the waiter and scanned the listings before her. The letters blurred, and she squinted to read them rather than fish her glasses from her purse.

"See anything that looks good? Let me rephrase that: *Can* you see anything that looks good?"

She laughed and wrinkled her nose playfully at him. "I'll have the cheese omelet, smart-aleck."

"And I'll have the club sandwich and cheese soup," Whit ordered, sending the waiter away.

"I looked over the publicity schedule and it looks fine to me. I hope you understand that I'll need some time to myself to keep in touch with my office. It's important to keep the column up to date, and that means I'll have to dictate answers to letters we receive while I'm away."

"I understand. I'm a fan of your column."

"You are?" she asked, looking at him again and seeing the fun-loving football player she had known years ago.

"I am. It's my favorite part of the newspaper." He grew silent while the waiter placed their iced teas in front of them. "I'm glad you found a way to combine your sociology degree with your talent for writing."

She smiled and nodded. "So am I. That's not the best degree for making a living. I should have majored in communications, like you."

"Oh, you've done pretty well for yourself," Whit objected.

"So have you." She shook her head and laughed softly. "I always thought you'd try out for professional football."

"Me? Pro football? No way." He took a drink of tea before he continued. "They would have made mincemeat out of me. You have to be an animal to make one of those teams!"

The waiter arrived with Whit's soup, and Emmy took the opportunity to examine the stamp of maturity the years had given Whit since college. She'd been so surprised to see him yesterday that she'd barely glanced at him, but the shock had long since subsided, and seeing him again was unearthing a myriad of memories. It occurred to her that she hadn't paid much attention to him when he'd visited her home occasionally while she'd been married to Jerry. Whit had just been one of Jerry's golfing buddies, and she'd forgotten until now how much time she'd spent with Whit in college.

She recalled how envious her girlfriends had been of her working day in and day out with Whit, but she'd been so wrapped up in Jerry that she'd never thought of Whit in romantic terms. He'd been just a coworker, but she'd enjoyed his companionship, especially his gentle teasing and ribald sense of humor.

The years since college had etched laugh lines at the corners of his eyes and deepened the grooves at the sides of his mouth. His sandy blond hair was thick and wavy, and carefully combed into a side part, but Emmy remembered its being unruly and, more often than not, tousled and windblown. His eyes were a warm, deep shade of brown as intoxicating as sherry. He wore a gray double-breasted suit, white shirt and silvery gray tie. The clothes added a new dimension, since Emmy couldn't remember ever seeing him dressed in anything other than casual wear. These were things strangers would notice about Whit, but those more familiar with him would see the subtleties such as his expressive, long-fingered hands, the kindness of his gaze and that devastating, lopsided grin that had made him infamous in college. Even Emmy had not been immune to that rakish twist of his lips. If she hadn't been so in love with Jerry she would have fallen prey to Whit's lethal weapon.

"What are you thinking about?" Whit asked, noticing that she was staring a hole through him.

Emmy averted her gaze and took a drink of the mint-flavored iced tea. "Oh, I was just wool-gathering about college. It seems so long ago that we worked together on the yearbook."

"It wasn't that long. I was looking through the annual a few days ago. We were a scruffy-looking bunch back then, weren't we?"

Emmy smiled, thinking of those days when jeans, T-shirts and clogs were the school uniform. "Yes, we were. I've noticed that college fashions are more conservative than they were when we were students."

"Do you still have your rimless glasses?"

The left side of his mouth slanted up, and Emmy felt that old, familiar tingle of attraction. He hadn't lost his touch, she thought. He was still heavily armed.

"I have them tucked away in a drawer, along with my peace-symbol T-shirt." A thread of sadness wove through her. "What happened to us? What became of all those fiery promises to change the world for the better?"

Whit shrugged, and she saw the sadness she felt settle in his eyes. He used his napkin to dab at a drop of cheese soup on his full lower lip before he answered. "We grew up, I guess. All wasn't lost. We *did* make people stop and think for a few years."

"I suppose so. I was going to help the poor and downtrodden, and here I am giving advice to the lovelorn."

"It's a worthy profession. As someone once said, 'The only abnormality is the incapacity to love.'"

Her gaze swept slowly to his, and she was relieved to see sincerity there. Years of living with a man who viewed her profession as quackery had made her defensive, and it was a pleasant change to be with a man who viewed it as worthwhile.

The waiter arrived with Emmy's omelet and Whit's sandwich. The food was attractively prepared. Emmy tasted the cheesy omelet and smiled her appreciation to the waiter before he hurried to another table.

"Nonfiction books such as yours do very well in the market," Whit said, abruptly returning the conversation to business. "Your book is coming out at a good time, too. People emerge from their winter hibernation and head for the bookstores."

"Yes, my publisher mentioned that. What kinds of questions will I be asked during interviews?"

"Just the basics, I imagine. Television interviewers have very little time, so they generally stick to the facts. Where can the book be purchased, how much does it cost, how long did it take to write it, and do you have a favorite letter? That sort of thing."

"I can handle that."

He smiled and gave her a wink. "I know you can. I'll brief you before each interview, so you'll know what to expect."

"Do you like being your own boss now?"

"I love it."

"Do you have a large list of clients?"

"A large list?" He paused to think while he finished his soup. "We could use a few more, but we're satisfied. We've represented authors, companies and products, so we've established ourselves as being versatile." He took a bite of his sandwich, and Emmy watched his Adam's apple move slowly in his tanned throat when he swallowed. "I must admit that I'm the best boss I've ever had. I give myself two-hour lunches occasionally, and raises frequently."

"Doesn't Pete Bitters have something to say about that?"

"We have a company motto. 'If it isn't broken, don't fix it.' In other words, as long as the business makes money, we stay out of each other's way."

"Where did you meet Pete?"

"We worked for the same PR company before we decided to join forces and open our own firm."

"And the rest is history," Emmy said with a smile, admiring his ambition and professional courage. Starting a business was risky. Emmy remembered how terrified she'd been when her column was syndicated and she'd realized that she had become a business. "Was it just a wild coincidence that you were hired to represent me?"

He glanced at her, and she wondered if he could sense her suspicion. "No, not really. Pete and Tom Griven are old friends. I heard that ACTION was looking for a PR firm, and I told Pete to get the account."

"Why?"

"Because I wanted it."

"Why?"

His glance was pointed this time. "To make money, of course."

"That's it?"

He pushed aside the remains of his sandwich as if he'd suddenly lost his appetite. "What other motive would I have had?"

"You tell me," Emmy goaded, sensing his uneasiness with the line of questioning and wanting to know its source.

His dark blond brows lowered, and he sat back in his chair to glower at her. "What's on your mind, Emmy? I don't like playing twenty questions."

"Skip it." She directed her attention to the waiter, who had arrived to clean off their table. "Could I have a cup of coffee with cream, please?"

"Make that two," Whit said.

"Two coffees with cream," the waiter repeated before leaving them alone again.

Whit shifted in his chair restlessly. "I've brought you up to date about myself; now it's your turn. How's life been treating you?" His tone was friendly again, but Emmy could sense that he was still edgy from her persistent questioning.

"I'm sure you know all about me from Jerry." She challenged him with an unwavering gaze.

"I'd rather hear it from you."

"I'm not complaining." She looked around the restaurant as her anger returned. She had every right to complain, she thought. Divorce was horrible enough without having it drag on for years.

"That's it?" He crossed his arms on the table and leaned forward. "Why do I get the feeling that you don't trust me?"

"You said yesterday that you haven't seen Jerry for a while."

"That's right."

She fished around for a diplomatic way to speak her mind while the waiter set cups of coffee before them. She finally decided on the direct approach. "I'm trying very hard to get Jerry out of my life, Whit. I'm not crazy about the idea of working with you."

"Why not? I told you that—"

"You're Jerry's friend," she cut in. "It's only natural that you'd talk to Jerry about me, and I don't want Jerry to know about my business dealings."

His sigh was laden with frustration, and he looked away from her. In profile his face riveted her attention. His square jaw was rock-hard with determination, and his full lips were tense with impatience. Emmy sipped her coffee and waited for him to tamp down his anger.

"You think I'd run to Jerry and tell him every little thing you said and did while we were together?" He glanced sideways at her, and his look had a cutting edge. "Is that why you thought I wanted your account?"

"Well, I . . . it crossed my mind." She flinched involuntarily when he faced her and released the full impact of his furious glare.

"It crossed your mind," he repeated with a smirk. "It never crossed mine. I wanted to work with you because I like you. It has nothing to do with Jerry."

"I'm sorry." Emmy waved a dismissing hand. "Let's just drop it."

"Would you rather have Pete represent you?"

It seemed like a sensible solution, but it didn't appeal to her. Whit hadn't done her any harm, she argued with herself. She was jumping to conclusions, and that was unfair to Whit. The least she could do was give him a chance to prove his integrity.

"No," she answered, and thought she saw a measure of relief in his expression. "Let's play it by ear."

"I'm good at my job, Emmy." He finished his coffee and signed the check. "You know, I always thought I was as much your friend as Jerry's. In fact, if you're dividing up your friends, I'd rather be part of your side of the settlement."

Emmy smiled and reached for her purse. "We're not dividing up our friends. You and I used to be good friends in college, didn't we? I guess we grew apart while I was married."

"We can remedy that now. I'd like to be your good friend again."

She wanted to believe him, but there was still a shadow of doubt in her mind. She cleared her throat and decided to stick to business.

"Is there anything I should do in preparation for the autograph party next week?"

"Just practice your signature." He grinned, and the warmth was back in his eyes. "You'll feel just like a movie star."

"I doubt that."

"I'll set up everything at the bookstore. All you have to do is show up on time and bring a pen."

"And smile a lot, I suppose."

"That's right. Are you looking forward to the publicity tour or are you dreading it?"

"A little bit of both, I guess."

"It will be fun, Emmy." He stood up and helped her from her chair, taking her elbow lightly as they made their way to the front of the restaurant. "You'll get to visit different cities and meet all kinds of people."

"I won't have time to sight-see, will I?"

"We'll make time." He opened the door for her, then followed her outside. "Need a ride back to your office?"

"Yes, thanks."

"Then you'd better hail a taxi." He grinned mischievously when she whirled to face him, her eyes widening at his rudeness. "Just kidding, just kidding," he said with a chuckle. "My car is parked over here in the lot."

Emmy laughed with him. "I'd forgotten how you love to rattle people. I guess I'll have to be on my toes around you."

"If I remember correctly, you never had much trouble keeping up with or even besting me." He indicated a white Jaguar. "Pretty snazzy, huh?"

"This is yours?"

"Mine and the bank's." He opened the passenger door and helped her into the low sports car before going around to the other side and folding his tall frame behind the leather-wrapped steering wheel.

Emmy breathed in the earthy scent of leather laced

with the spicy after-shave Whit wore. "Ummm. This car smells delicious."

"Beats the smell of taxi cabs, doesn't it?"

"By a mile," Emmy agreed. "I guess this cost a pretty penny."

"It's worth it." He steered the car from the lot and merged with the congested Atlanta traffic. "Have you ever been to any of the cities we'll be visiting?"

"I've never been to Miami or Knoxville, but I passed through New Orleans once. I zipped through the French Quarter, but I didn't get to really see anything there."

"What a shame! You mean you didn't stop for coffee and donuts at the Café du Monde?"

"No, but I've heard of it."

"It's legendary. We'll have to put it on our itinerary."

She glanced at him, thinking that it sounded as if they were planning a vacation instead of a business trip. She smiled, thinking of his teasing sense of humor and silently thanking him for making her laugh and forget her nagging problems with Jerry. Her smile slipped from her lips when she thought of Jerry and the appeal. Was Whit really her friend, or was he still pals with Jerry? She wanted to believe that she could trust Whit, but there was a shadow of a doubt lurking deep within her that only time could erase.

"This is my office building," Emmy said as her fingers wrapped around the door handle. "Just let me out in front and I'll—"

"Can't I come in?" Whit asked. "I'd like to see your office."

"Well, I guess so. There's not much to see. It's just your basic desks, chairs, plants and filing cabinets."

"I'd still like to see where Maudie does her work."

"Okay," Emmy said with a shrug. "I don't think Maudie would mind."

Whit parked the car in the lot behind the building. "Why in the world did your mother name you Maude Edith? Had she no heart?"

"She has plenty of heart, and two sisters who mean the world to her."

"Namely Maude and Edith?" Whit asked as he helped her from the car.

"That's right."

"What's your mother's name?"

Emmy giggled. "Inez."

Whit rolled his eyes heavenward. "Your grandmother is the real culprit." He rested the flat of his hand between her shoulder blades as they entered the building. "However, I like the name Emmy. Was that your mother's idea?"

"My father's, bless his good taste." Emmy led the way to the elevator, and Whit's hand slipped from her back. His touch had been warm, making Emmy agonizingly aware of his virile presence. "We're on the sixth floor."

"We?"

"I have an assistant. You'll love her. Everybody does."

The elevator doors opened, and Emmy crossed the hall and flung open the door marked "Ask Maudie, Inc." Bertha looked up from her cluttered desk with an automatic smile that intensified when she spotted Whit.

"Hello, Emmy."

"Hi, Bert. Bertha, this is Whittier Hayes, co-owner of Town Crier Public Relations. Whit, this is my indispensable assistant, Bertha Glasser."

"Nice to meet you, Mrs. Glasser." Whit shook Bertha's hand. "This must be an interesting job."

"Oh, it is, and please call me Bertha."

"And I'm Whit."

"Whit." Bertha grinned and patted her carrot red hair into place. "We don't get many visitors in here other than the mailman, so please excuse my appearance."

Standing behind Whit, Emmy looked past his shoulder and wagged a finger at Bertha. What a flirt, she thought. Bertha never passed up a chance to flutter her pale orange lashes at a handsome man. She even had the ferret-faced mailman thinking he was Don Juan.

"You look lovely, so there's no need to make excuses for yourself, Bertha." Whit examined the stacks of letters on Bertha's and Emmy's desks and issued a low whistle. "Do you answer all of these?"

"No, that would be impossible," Emmy said, picking up one of them and squinting at the nearly illegible handwriting. "Many of the problems are identical, so we select one that represents a common problem and answer it."

"And then there are always a few that are unique," Bertha said, drawing Whit's attention back to her. "For the most part, however, we can file them under listings like 'Jealousy,' 'Two-timers,' 'Sexual Aberrations' and that sort of thing."

"That last one sounds interesting," Whit said, joining in Bertha's flirtations.

"You bet," Bertha agreed. "Most of those we can't print in a family newspaper."

Whit chuckled and turned to Emmy. "Has Maudie ever received any marriage proposals through the mail?"

"Maudie? Heavens, no!" Emmy laughed, finding the idea ludicrous.

"After this publicity tour, she might." Whit picked up

one of the letters, started to read it, then dropped it as if it were a hot coal. He cleared his throat and faced Emmy again. "When men discover that Maudie is a lovely, available woman, watch out!"

"I never thought about that," Emmy said with a slight frown.

"I hope I get to read those letters," Bertha said with a burst of throaty giggles.

Whit looked around the tastefully appointed office and gave a sharp nod. "This reflects you, Emmy. Muted earth tones with touches of pastel, and an emphasis on organization and efficiency." He spotted her word processor and moved over to it for a closer look. "This beats a typewriter all to heck, doesn't it?"

"Yes, but it's a relatively new addition to the office. I've had it less than a year, and I can't imagine how I ever lived without it."

"I know what you mean." He straightened from his inspection of the machine and looked at the clock. "Is that clock right?"

"Yes," Emmy answered, then stared at it in amazement. Had she been with Whit for more than two hours?

"I didn't know it was so late." Whit extended his hand to Bertha again. "It was nice flirting with you, Bertha."

Bertha blushed and waved her hand in a shooing motion. "Oh, you devil! Do you have to leave so soon?" She asked, slipping her big-boned hand into Whit's.

"I'm afraid so. I've whiled away enough of the afternoon." He squeezed Bertha's hand, released it, and turned back to Emmy. "It was a pleasure, Emmy. I'll be seeing you again soon."

"Okay. Thanks for the lunch, and give my regards to Pete."

"I will." His warm gaze rested on her face for several moments, making her body temperature soar. His slight smile was private and unnerving. "I hope I set things straight between us."

Emmy nodded, preferring to be as noncommittal as possible for the time being. "See you later, Whit."

"Right." He drew himself up as if emerging from a mild trance, flicked his hand in a choppy wave and left the office.

"Whew!" Bertha fell back in her chair in a feigned swoon. "What a dreamboat! Be still my heart." Her hand fluttered over her breast.

"Grab hold of yourself," Emmy cautioned with a laugh. "You're a married woman, remember?"

"I'm married, but I'm not dead!" Bertha looked up at the ceiling and a delicious smile floated across her face. "Lordy, lordy! What a hunk. Tell me he's single."

"He's single."

She opened her eyes wide. "And the way he looked at you!"

"What look?"

"Right before he left," she explained breathlessly. "He gave you a look you could have poured over a waffle."

"Oh, Bertha!" Emmy spun around to conceal the wave of embarrassment that swept up over her face. "You're seeing things." She sat down behind her desk and switched on the word processor. "All he's interested in is the money he can make off my book."

"Baloney. Is that the man you met yesterday for cocktails?"

"One of them. I've known Whit since college."

"You have? You mean you let him slip through your fingers?"

"It wasn't like that. He was Jerry's friend."

"Oh." Bertha wrinkled her nose. "I would have thought Whit had better taste than that."

Emmy slanted Bertha a teasing look and hissed like a cat. "That wasn't very nice, Bertha. Jerry was one of the most popular guys on campus."

"What about Whit? What was he like back then?"

"He was quarterback of the football team and . . . well, he had quite a reputation with the girls."

"I just bet he did," Bertha said with a wicked laugh. "And I bet he earned it. You're a lucky woman, Emmy."

"Lucky? What do you mean?"

"You're going to be spending a lot of time with that handsome brute. That's better than winning a two-week paid vacation to Hawaii!"

Emmy rolled her eyes and faced the word processor again, but Bertha's words found their mark. She *would* be spending time with Whit, and she had to admit that Bertha had a point. Whittier Hayes was a very attractive man.

3

Dear T.C.,

Sorry to hear of your less than successful reunion with Susie. You failed to mention your association with her ex-husband in your first letter, and this adds a definite wrinkle to your relationship with her.

Divorce is a battlefield of broken promises, distrust and personal failure. You must give Susie time to put these things behind her. Why not throw a party and invite her? She might not be comfortable yet with one-on-one dating situations, and a party with other people around will put her at ease and give you a chance to show off your sterling qualities.

I'm on your side, and I'm sure Susie will be soon, so hang in there.

Maudie

Bertha folded the morning newspaper and smiled across the office at Emmy.

"What is it?" Emmy asked, noticing Bertha's pleased expression.

"I like Torch Carrier," Bertha said, pointing to the "Ask Maudie" column in the newspaper. "He sounds like a nice guy. Isn't it touching that he's still in love with Susie after all these years?"

"Yes," Emmy agreed, pushing her chair back from the word processor and resting her chin in her palm. "I hope my advice does the trick for him this time. Poor T.C. sounds as if he's suffering."

"I think your idea of a party is inspired. It's tough to start dating again after you've been faithful to one man for years." Bertha glanced at the column once more before turning her attention to the unopened mail. "You've been quiet this morning. Something troubling you?"

Emmy smiled in wonder at Bertha's keen sixth sense and removed her oval-shaped reading glasses. "I can't ever fool you, can I? Yes, something is bothering me."

"What is it? I'm all ears."

Emmy plucked a tissue from its decorative box and began cleaning the lenses of her glasses. "The same old thing."

"Jerry," Bertha said without hesitation.

"On the nose."

"What's he done now?"

Emmy glanced up from her task and issued a long, exasperated sigh. "The couple interested in buying my house is getting cold feet. My real estate agent explained this court appeal and that I can't sell the house until it's settled. They've asked to see other houses, so it looks as if I'm going to be stuck with my white elephant for a while longer."

"Oh, Em, I'm sorry to hear that," Bertha said sympathetically. "I know how anxious you are to sell the house. Can't your attorney light a fire under one of the judges and get this appeal thing settled quickly?"

"He's trying, but the court docket is full, and the wheels of justice need oiling."

"Tell me about it," Bertha said, rolling her eyes. "My nephew has been trying to collect on an automobile acci—" Bertha chopped off her sentence when the phone rang. She arched her brows and pointed to herself. "You want me to—"

"I'll answer it," Emmy said, picking up the receiver. " 'Ask Maudie.' Emmy speaking."

"Whit speaking."

Emmy smiled as the sound of Whit's voice miraculously brightened her mood. "Well, hello. I was beginning to think you'd fallen off the face of the earth."

"Were you?" His pleased chuckle floated across the line. "I've been working on your account."

"I haven't heard from you in almost a week, and I thought you might have decided to let Pete handle my publicity."

"No, nothing like that. I've just been busy. As a matter of fact, I'm calling to remind you of that party we've scheduled Saturday evening to officially launch your book."

"Yes, I haven't forgotten. Seven o'clock at the Peachtree—"

"Correction," Whit interrupted. "I had to change the location because of a printing mix-up. My secretary sent out the invitations listing my house as the location of the party."

"Your house?"

"Yes." He sighed expansively. "It's a long story."

"Did you fire her?" Emmy asked, a smile in her voice.

"No. It was an honest mistake. Anyway, the party will be at my place, and I'll send a car to pick you up."

"Oh, that's nice. Do you live in the city?"

"No, I live outside it in Flowery Branch."

"I know where that is," Emmy said. "I have a girl-friend who used to live there. This must be an imposition."

"No, I don't mind. I like to entertain. Several members of the Atlanta media will be there, as well as people from ACTION."

"I'm getting nervous."

"Don't. Just look at this as a chance to make new friends. I'll see you tomorrow night at seven, okay?"

"Okay. Thanks for calling and reminding me. 'Bye now."

" 'Bye, Emmy."

Emmy replaced the receiver and grinned at Bertha's bright-eyed expression. "Yes, that was Whit," she answered Bertha's unasked question.

"You're going to a party at his house?"

"Yes, but it's strictly business."

"He seems like a nice man, Emmy."

Noting Bertha's serious tone, Emmy nodded. "He is."

"Was he nice in college, too?"

Emmy sat back in her chair and relaxed, letting her thoughts travel back to her co-ed days. "I always thought

Whit was attractive in college, but I believe he's more handsome now than he was then. Age has done wonderful things to him." She recalled the lines that fanned out from the corners of his eyes, and a quiet wisdom that had not been so apparent in college.

"Is he anything like Jerry? I mean, they are friends, and like usually attracts like."

"No, he's not like Jerry." Emmy shrugged. "Of course, I sort of lost touch with Whit after graduation. He dropped by the house every so often to pick up Jerry for a game of golf, but I never talked to him very much. There was a time when I thought Whit might have a good influence on Jerry." She smiled at her foolish thoughts. "You know, I thought Whit's common sense might rub off on him. Whit always had a good head on his shoulders."

"I'll say!" Bertha giggled mischievously. "Speaking of good heads, I bet he turned a few in college."

Emmy laughed with Bertha. "He was a heartthrob, that's for sure."

"Does he still see Jerry?"

Emmy's laughter died abruptly as Bertha touched on her secret concern. "He says he doesn't."

"But you don't believe him?" Bertha asked, her sixth sense kicking in again.

"I don't know," Emmy said, her tone fraught with indecision as she slipped her glasses back on. "He insists that he doesn't see him anymore, but Whit's association with Jerry bothers me."

"Why?"

"Because I know how men gossip, that's why. I'm afraid that Whit will talk to Jerry about my business dealings, and it's none of Jerry's concern."

"Oh, I get the picture." Bertha stroked her double chin thoughtfully. "Did you tell Whit how you felt?"

"Yes, and he was understandably miffed. He said he was on my side and that he wouldn't disclose personal information like that to anyone."

"But you're still not convinced?"

Emmy shook her head, feeling guilty for still distrusting Whit. "What do you think, Bertha? Should I take him at his word?"

Bertha pushed herself from her chair and walked slowly to the coffee machine for a refill. "I'll tell you what I think, honey. I think it's a good idea to treat folks the way you'd like to be treated."

Emmy's guilty feelings reached a new height. "You're right. I should be more trusting, I guess."

"Play it by ear, Emmy," Bertha advised as she stirred three cubes of sugar into her coffee. "Trust your instincts."

"What do your instincts tell you?" Emmy asked, trusting Bertha's keen instincts more than her own.

Bertha turned to face Emmy, and her chocolate brown eyes crinkled at the corners. "My instincts tell me that you like Whit and that he likes you, and that that bothers you more than his friendship with Jerry."

Emmy felt heat rush up her neck and into her cheeks, and she looked away from Bertha's all too perceptive gaze. "I . . . that's . . . oh, Bert! Really!"

Bertha's giggles floated across to Emmy, speaking more eloquently than words.

Whit's home was the type of house Emmy had wanted when Jerry had insisted on buying a monstrosity that had quickly become an albatross around Emmy's neck. The house was located in a quiet subdivision in the neighboring community of Flowery Branch, less than an hour's drive from bustling Atlanta. It was a commuter's dream; treed lots with manicured lawns and wide, paved streets served as backdrops for homes of brick and timber. Whit's house was situated in a cul-de-sac and was red brick with slate-colored trim.

The rooms were large enough for a small gathering of friends and associates, but small enough to keep tidy without hiring domestic help. About twenty people had been invited to the party, most of them members of the media. Wearing a conservative after-five dress of charcoal silk, Emmy stood in the center of the living room and listened to three television anchors discuss the advantages and disadvantages of being minor celebrities. Whit and Tom Griven were across the room from her and deep in discussion. Whit's expressive hands punctuated his side of the conversation, and Tom laughed at something Whit said, then shook a stubby finger at him in a playful rebuke.

Whit looked particularly attractive in a teal blue suit, cream shirt and striped tie. His hair was combed into its side part, and Emmy's fingers itched to muss it. Although his suit was well tailored, Emmy thought that he looked better in jeans and sports shirts. There was something earthy about him, something that was stunted when he wore suits, ties and dress shirts.

Emmy felt boredom seep through her like a potent tranquilizer and she glanced at the empty glass in her hand, then seized the excuse that she needed to replenish her drink.

"Excuse me," Emmy said, cutting into the tedious discussion of film versus tape, "but I need a refill. No, that's okay," she said, removing her glass from the reach of one of the men. "I'll get it myself, thanks."

Congratulating herself on her escape from the circle, she made her way to the kitchen. Louvered doors separated it from the living room, and Emmy breathed a sigh of relief when she entered the quiet sanctum. Three hours of polite conversation had become tedious, and she welcomed the chance to be alone for a few minutes.

She went to the combination refrigerator/freezer for ice, but took the opportunity to check out its contents. By the amount of food stored in both sides, she surmised that Whit cooked at home a lot instead of going out. She dropped a couple of ice cubes into her glass and reached for the bottle of soda on one of the shelves. She'd had a glass too much of vodka and tonic, and she craved something nonalcoholic. The lemony-lime soda was just the ticket, and she hoped Whit wouldn't mind that she had helped herself to his provisions.

The faint hum of conversation in the next room made her cool her heels a while longer. She leaned against the counter and soaked in the cheery color combination of yellow and orange. The oak table in the center of the tiled floor was big enough for four and looked antique. The matching chairs had shocks of wheat carved in the rounded backs, and their needlepoint cushions added bright splashes of rust, brown, yellow and blue flowers. Her fingers moved unerringly up to the collar of her dress where a small bundle of blue and white forget-me-nots was pinned. Whit had presented them to her when she'd arrived, surprising her with his thoughtfulness.

He'd introduced her to everyone, then melted into the background, but she was constantly aware of his presence. He was never more than a few feet from her, and it was a comfort to know that he was nearby. Discussion of her book had dominated the conversations for the first hour, but the guests had tired of the subject and broken into smaller groups to discuss foreign subjects such as video cameras, television news programs and the invasion of computers in newspaper and magazine production. It had worried Emmy that the media had soon tired of her upcoming book publicity, but Whit had taken her aside and explained that it was natural for the hometown media to show a lack of enthusiasm for their own celebrities.

"You'll have to make a splash in other cities before the Atlanta reporters take notice," Whit had explained with a baffled shrug. "Familiarity breeds contempt, as they say, and these people won't pay much attention until their counterparts in other cities start singing your praises; then they'll start clamoring for interviews."

His explanation had enlightened her and made her more aware of his knowledge and abilities. It would be useful to have Whit on her side when she traipsed across the South in search of recognition. Her connection with the public had been limited to the written word, but Whit was accustomed to dealing with the public in a more personal way.

Emmy jumped slightly as a sound interrupted her reverie. She looked to the louvered door automatically, thinking that her refuge had been invaded, but found no one there. Positive that she had heard something, she held her breath and listened intently. The sound came again, faint and low-pitched. It wasn't human.

Zeroing in on the disturbance, Emmy went to the folding door beside the refrigerator. She pushed it back and stared at the washer, dryer and shelves of laundry products. Nothing here, she thought. She started to close the door when movement caught her eye, and she stepped inside the room toward a wicker laundry basket. She looked inside and gasped when she saw the dark-colored cat amid the bundle of soiled clothing.

"What's this?" Emmy crouched beside the basket, wanting to stroke the cat, but thinking better of it. "Are you hurt?"

The cat looked at her with dull, green eyes and mewed plaintively. She stretched out on her side, and Emmy saw that the cat was very pregnant.

"You're not having babies, are you?"

The cat's tail swished, and she mewed again, the sound filled with discomfort.

"Yes, I think you are," Emmy said as she stood up. She felt helpless. She took a sip of her drink and wondered if she should alert Whit to the situation.

"Emmy?"

Emmy whirled toward Whit's voice. "I'm in your laundry room."

"The laundry room?" He entered her field of vision, a perplexed expression on his lean face. "Does it meet with your approval?"

"There's a very pregnant cat in here who is in the throes of labor."

"What?" He was beside her in a shot and wasted no time in dropping to his haunches beside the basket and stroking the cat's head and bulging side. "Elda, you have lousy timing. Couldn't you have waited until tomorrow? I'm having a party!"

"What did you call her?" Emmy asked, crouching next to him.

"Elda, short for Esmerelda."

Emmy threw him a startled glance. "And you made fun of my grandmother's taste in names? Shame on you."

The concern on his face was swept aside for a moment, and he smiled. "I guess that is a little like the pot calling the kettle black." He laid a hand on the cat's stomach, and Emmy saw his fingers being lifted by the squirming bodies inside. "Poor Esmerelda," Whit crooned in a tone Emmy had not heard from him before. "Does it hurt?" He looked at Emmy. "What can I do to help her?"

Emmy smiled, thinking that Whit was adorable. "I guess you could time her contractions, but I don't think that will help her very much. I think the best thing would be to let her do her thing and just keep an eye on her in case she has a problem."

"I think she already has a problem. Listen to her; she's crying, isn't she?"

"I believe that sound is closer to groaning or moaning. Don't you think we should go back to our guests?"

"I hate to leave her." Whit looked over his shoulder, then back to his pet. "You think she'll be okay?"

"For the time being, yes. Once we get rid of everybody, I'll stay until the crisis is over."

"Thanks." He looked positively relieved. "I've never been through this before."

Emmy laughed and placed her hand on his shoulder for support as she rose to her feet. "I haven't either."

"Yes, but women know more about these things."

"That's what men keep telling us," Emmy said with a touch of sarcasm. "Come on, Whit. She'll be okay."

He patted the cat's head once more before rising to his feet and accompanying Emmy back to the living room. Emmy whiled away another hour talking with the guests and receiving their polite congratulations on her upcoming book, but she noticed that Whit's attention was divided between his chattering guests and the kitchen door. She knew he was relieved when the guests began leaving around ten o'clock, and she wondered if they noticed that their host was giving them a subtle version of the bum's rush.

When Whit closed the door behind the last guest he reached for Emmy's hand and pulled her toward the kitchen.

"I'm sorry about this, Emmy. Elda's spoiled the party for me."

"It's not your fault," Emmy consoled him as she followed him into the laundry room and over to the wicker basket.

"Oh, my gosh! Will you look at this?" Whit's voice was filled with excitement and an undercurrent of wonder. He sat cross-legged beside the basket and awe bathed his face.

Emmy dropped to her knees beside him and caught her breath when she spotted two bundles of wet fur—one white and one mottled brown. "How cute! She's been busy while we've been in the living room."

"It *was* that white tom cat," Whit said, touching the white ball of fur. "I suspected as much."

"You don't sound pleased."

Whit shrugged his shoulders and the tip of his finger stroked one tiny, white paw. "I'd made an appointment with the veterinarian to spay her, but before I could get her to the vet I came home one day to find a screen ripped off one of my windows."

"Breaking and entering?" Emmy asked.

"Something like that. When I took Elda to the vet I was informed that she was pregnant. They suggested an abortion, but I couldn't do that to Elda." He shook his finger at the exhausted cat. "Naughty girl. I bet you

56

encouraged him. In fact, I bet you helped him tear off the screen." He chuckled under his breath and looked at Emmy. "She had been looking through the windows and flirting with a stray tom cat, a big, white, scruffy-looking hombre." He touched the white kitten again. "Like father, like son . . . or daughter."

"What are you going to do with the kittens?"

"Find homes for them." Whit patted Elda's smooth head affectionately. "Do you think she's finished?"

"Not by a long shot. I think we should make a pot of coffee and get comfortable. This could take hours."

"Hours?" He frowned and glared at Elda, who was cleaning her babies. "Can't you move faster than that, Elda?"

"Have a heart, Whit," Emmy scolded as she stood up and started for the kitchen. "You can't rush Mother Nature. Where's your coffee?"

"I'll make it." Whit pushed himself up and went to the cabinet over the sink. "You don't have to stay if you'd rather not."

"I want to." Emmy sat at the kitchen table and smiled at him when he turned to face her.

"Thanks. How about a midnight snack? I've got crackers and cheese."

"Sounds delicious. Where did you get Esmerelda?"

"A friend gave her to me for Christmas two years ago."

"A female friend?" Emmy asked, keeping her gaze locked on the flower arrangement in the center of the table.

"Yes. She moved to Chicago last year."

Emmy fingered one of the silk flowers and felt Whit's alert gaze on her. "That's too bad."

"That's life. People come and go." He went to the refrigerator for a platter of cheese which he set on the table along with a box of crackers. "Help yourself."

"Do you miss her?" Emmy asked, opening the box and removing a few of the crackers.

"I wasn't in love with her."

Her fingers tensed, and one of the crackers crumbled in her hand. She forced herself to face him with a nonchalant shrug. "I didn't mean to pry." But I am, she added silently, wondering why she was so intent on knowing how often and whom he dated.

"I dated her off and on for a couple of years, but it wasn't serious."

"Do you like to date?"

"I don't have much choice." He laughed softly and plugged in the coffeepot. "It's either that or celibacy, and I prefer the former to the latter."

"I dread the very thought of dating again," Emmy said on a sigh. "It makes me nervous."

"Nervous?" Whit said with a chuckle as he sat down at the table with her. He selected a sliver of cheese and placed it between two crackers. "Why would dating make you nervous?"

"Oh, all the production that goes into it. You meet someone, he asks you out, you worry about what to wear and what to say and where to go and . . ." She flipped her hand and groaned. "And everything!"

Whit bit into the cracker and cheese, then swept crumbs off his tie. "Don't worry. I'll make it easy for you."

"What?" She looked at him, confused and bewildered. "What do you mean?"

Whit hooked one elbow over the back of his chair, and

a lazy smile touched his lips. "I'll pick you up next Saturday at eleven o'clock and we'll go to Helen for some sight-seeing. Wear something comfortable, like jeans. Topics of conversation will be you, me and the things we see along the way," he said, ticking them off on his fingers. "I'll spring for lunch, and we might even have dinner before we wander back to Atlanta. Any questions?"

Emmy stared at him dumbfounded for a few seconds before she managed to force a question past her lips. "Are you asking me for a date?"

He narrowed his eyes thoughtfully and nodded. "By George, I think she's got it!" Whit leaned forward in sudden concern. "Are you nervous already?"

Emmy laughed and slapped his arm playfully. "Stop it. You're not the first man to ask me out since my divorce, you know."

"I never presumed I was," Whit said, his expressive eyes losing some of their teasing light. "Anyone can look at you and know that. Did you accept any of those dates?"

"A couple," Emmy said, frowning a little when she remembered the stilted conversations and her utter relief when the evenings were over.

"From the look on your face, I gather you didn't enjoy the experiences."

"They made me swear off dating," Emmy admitted.

"Can't I change your mind? We're not strangers. We have a lot in common." His hand moved across the table and covered hers. "Have you been to Helen?"

"Yes, years ago. It's lovely." Looking into his eyes and feeling his gentle touch swayed her to his side. "It might be fun."

"It *will* be fun," Whit promised. "Satisfaction guaranteed." He looked over his shoulder at the coffeepot when it gurgled to a stop. "Cream and sugar?"

"Just cream."

He poured the coffee and set the cups on the table along with a cream pitcher. "I think I'll peek in on Elda."

Emmy went into the laundry room with him. Elda had added another kitten to the litter; a black one with white paws and a blazed face.

"Where did this one come from?" Whit asked, obviously perplexed by the variety of Elda's brood.

"That white tom had a colorful lineage." Emmy took one of Whit's hands in hers and tugged him back toward the kitchen. "She's doing fine. Nothing to worry about."

They returned to their chairs at the kitchen table and sipped the coffee. Elda's soft mewing floated into the kitchen, making her owner cast a worried look toward the laundry room.

"There's nothing you can do, Whit," Emmy said, trying to read his thoughts.

"I was just wondering which of my friends I might be able to talk into taking a kitten."

"Bertha would adopt one," Emmy said, remembering that Bertha had mentioned recently that she thought she might get a pet. "And I think that white one is adorable."

Whit faced her, and a tender smile touched his lips. "It's yours." He held her hand again, and his fingers moved over her ring finger. "You charmed everyone tonight, including me." His eyes met hers briefly, then returned to her ring finger. "Will you go to Helen with me next weekend?"

"Yes." She smiled when he looked at her with obvious surprise. "Your carefully planned itinerary sold me."

His smile was slow and honeyed as he brought her

fingers up to his lips. Emmy tingled under the assault of his soft, moist kisses. He turned her hand over and pressed his mouth to her palm, and his gaze lifted to hers, creating a simmering in her heart. The chemical attraction was strong, much stronger than Emmy could have imagined. The play of his lips across her palm and wrist sent a weakness through her that Emmy hadn't felt in a long time. She realized that she had missed the sensation of falling under the spell of a man. The last time she had felt like this was when she was falling in love with Jerry.

Whit's other hand swept to the back of her neck, pulling her toward the magnetism of his parted lips. Emmy closed her eyes a split second before Whit's mouth settled on hers. There was a tough tenderness about the way he claimed her mouth, as if he wanted to be gentle but could barely keep himself in check.

His desire blew through her like a hot wind, raking her with fiery passion and fanning the burning embers of longing. His hand moved down the curve of her spine, drawing her closer to the fire storm of his touch, and his lips inched hers apart with probing expertise. Emmy knew she was in the arms of an expert seducer, and she gave herself up to the experience. The tip of his tongue wet her lips before moving inside in a slick caress as his hands wandered up and down her back. When his mouth left hers to trail down the side of her neck, Emmy drove her fingers through his hair, releasing it from its strict styling. She opened her eyes to view her masterpiece and emerged from her self-absorption before her selfish needs could transport her to a mindless state of passion.

Gently she extracted herself from the circle of his arms and managed a shaky laugh.

"We're getting a little carried away," she whispered.

Whit's gaze was too intense, and she looked toward the laundry room for a ready excuse. "We'd better check on Elda."

"Emmy," Whit said, his hand closing on her wrist to keep her in place, "don't run away."

"I'm not running away." She stared at the long fingers that held her prisoner.

"I want you. Don't you want me?"

"Not now." Emmy met his gaze boldly and tried not to evade the issue. "Not like this. It's too soon, and I'm not ready for it."

"Haven't you ever wanted to be swept away . . . swept off your feet?" He was teasing again, letting her off the hook.

"Only in my dreams," Emmy said, grateful for his delicate handling of what could have been a sticky situation. "I like you, Whit, but I . . . well, I . . ."

"You don't have to make excuses," Whit said, rising to his feet and running his fingers through his mussed hair. "A woman always has the right to change her mind or say no." He tipped his head toward the laundry room. "I wish Elda had exercised that right. If she had, I wouldn't have a litter of kittens on my hands."

Emmy laughed and glanced at her wristwatch. "I think I'll check on Elda's progress once more, and then I have to be getting home."

"Your driver is outside."

"Has he been there all this time?" Emmy asked, appalled to have kept the man waiting.

"No. He was supposed to come back for you by eleven." Whit checked his own watch. "It's almost midnight, but I imagine he's still out there. He gets paid by the hour, so don't worry about him." Whit went into the living room and looked out the front window. "Yes, he's parked in the drive."

"I feel like Cinderella," Emmy said with a laugh. "I'm not used to such royal treatment."

"Get used to it." Whit came back into the kitchen and took one of Emmy's hands in his. "It will be fun spoiling you. Let's say good night to the little mother."

Esmerelda turned soulful green eyes up to them when they entered her nursery. One more kitten, this one a spitting image of its mother, had arrived, and Elda was busy cleaning it. The other kittens were nursing, their tiny paws instinctively pushing against their mother's stomach.

"They're so adorable," Emmy said, crouching beside the basket and touching the white kitten's squirming body. "I think she's finished."

"That makes four kittens. I sincerely hope she's finished." Whit stroked Elda's head lovingly. "Well done, Elda. You came through this like a trouper."

"Well, I'd better go. Every minute I stay, I'm costing you money." Emmy rose to her feet with Whit's hand at her elbow to steady her. "Thanks for an eventful evening. You really know how to show a girl a good time."

Whit chuckled and walked to the front door with her. "I'll keep a watchful eye on that white kitten for you."

"Please do. I haven't had a pet since I was sixteen, so I guess it's time for me to take on another one."

"They're good company." Whit's fingers closed more tightly on her elbow when she made a move to open the front door. "Of course, they can't hold a candle to human companionship." He dipped his head, and his lips brushed hers in a feathery farewell. "Good night, Emmy. Remember, next Saturday belongs to me."

"I'll remember. Good night."

Whit opened the door and stood on the threshold while Emmy went to the waiting limo and settled in its backseat. He was still standing in the doorway, silhouetted by the light, when Emmy looked back over her shoulder. The car turned a corner, and Emmy faced forward again, feeling light-headed and optimistic.

It had been an evening of beginnings, she thought with a smile, and that was a welcome change from the series of endings the past couple of years had brought her way. Her luck was changing, and it was long overdue.

4

Dear Maudie,

You are a lady and a scholar. Your advice did the trick and, thanks to you, Susie has agreed to go out with me.

The party idea was sheer genius. To be honest, Maudie, I'm a little scared now that my dream is so close to coming true. Any advice on how to handle this first, important date? I wish I could tell Susie how much she means to me, and how I've loved her since college, but I'm afraid such a confession would make her think that I'm driftier than a ten-cent compass.

What do you think? Should I wear my heart on my sleeve or hidden in my pocket?

Torch Carrier

Whit steered the sleek Jaguar around a bend and stomped on the brake. Ahead of the vehicle stretched a line of bumper-to-bumper cars, all threading their way into the picturesque town of Helen.

"Good grief!" Whit's eyes bulged and he craned his neck to glare at the congested traffic. "What's going on?"

"It was like this the last time I was here," Emmy said, recalling the trip several years ago. "How many miles are we from Helen?"

Whit glanced around to get his bearings. "A couple of miles, at least." His gaze moved to the rearview mirror and saw three other cars slip into line behind him. "We're stuck. The only way to go is forward—slowly."

Emmy laughed at Whit's soft moan. "We're in no hurry, are we?"

"No, I guess not." He shifted the car into first gear and drummed his lean fingers on the steering wheel. "I bet there's not an empty parking space in the whole town."

"We'll cross that bridge when we come to it," Emmy said, hoping to lighten his frustration at being embroiled in a traffic jam. "How's my kitten doing? Has she opened her eyes yet?"

"No, *he* hasn't."

"He?"

Whit nodded. "I'm pretty sure it's a male."

"I'll have to think of another name."

"What was your first choice?"

"Snow White," Emmy said, glancing at him to see his reaction. "She arrived on an enchanting night and . . ." She shrugged, seeing the beginnings of Whit's amused grin and losing the courage to level with him. "Anyway, that name won't do now."

"How about Prince Charming?" Whit asked with a lift of his brows.

"Prince Charming," Emmy said softly, trying out the name and liking the sound of it. "Yes, that would be in keeping with the theme, wouldn't it? Prince Charming it is."

"I'll inform him of that when I get home—correction, *if* I get home. We've moved all of an inch so far."

"Patience, Whit," Emmy said soothingly. "We'll get there eventually. Who will watch over Elda and her family while you're away?"

"Pete, I hope." The cars ahead moved, and Whit tromped down on the accelerator. The car jumped forward a few feet before Whit applied the brake again. "He's watched over Elda before, but I'm not sure he'll be crazy about taking in a litter of kittens."

"If he won't, Bertha will. By the way, she wants one of them."

"Good. Two down, two to go."

"Why don't you keep one as a playmate for Elda?"

"The thought's crossed my mind." A tender smile rested fleetingly on his lips. "That black one with the white paws and blazed face is a sweetheart. I think she likes me. She's the runt of the litter."

"Is she?" Emmy asked, transfixed by the gentle expression on his face and in his voice.

"Yes, and Elda seems to pay more attention to her than she does the others."

Emmy smiled as her gaze took in Whit's striking profile. His lashes were long and straight, shadowing eyes that held amber lights in their depths. The car eased forward with the traffic, and Emmy's attention was drawn to Whit's hands as they tightened on the wheel. Veins ran along the backs of them, creating an interesting pattern.

A memory broke loose and surfaced, bringing another smile to her lips. In her junior year in college, she had gone to the park for a picnic with the yearbook staff. Whit had grilled hamburgers for everyone, and Emmy could recall how cute he'd looked in a huge apron and floppy chef's hat. Later that day, Emmy had settled into one of the park swings, and Whit had pushed her toward the clouds. Suddenly his arms had come around her waist to hold her in mid-swing. His face had been close to hers, his lips an inch away, and Emmy had caught her breath at the longing that had poured through her. He had held her tightly to him for a few heart-stopping moments before cursing softly under his breath, releasing her and walking away. By the time Emmy had gathered her senses, Whit had already left the park. Everyone said he'd seemed angry or upset, even though he'd told them that he had to get back to the dorm and study for a test.

Emmy released the memory and studied the man beside her. That had been a strange encounter, she thought. What had she done to make him leave the picnic in such a hurry? Had he felt the same rush of longing she had?

"Ahoy!" Whit said, pointing straight ahead. "Thar she blows!"

Emmy laughed. "I told you we'd get there."

"We're not there yet." Whit tipped up his chin, trying to see over the cars ahead. "It's a madhouse. I'll be lucky to get in and out without someone ramming into my car."

"Are you sorry you suggested this outing?"

His attention snapped to her. "No. I'm just hungry, and I'd like to stretch my legs, but I'm glad you're here with me."

"So am I." Emmy let her gaze move over his red sports shirt, jeans and deck shoes. His hair was tousled, and he looked like the Whit of her memories. "I'm not even nervous."

"Why should you be? We're just two old friends sharing a Saturday." He shifted to a more relaxed position in the bucket seat, as if he'd resigned himself to the slow-moving traffic. "Read any good letters lately?"

"A few. Yesterday I received one from a lady in New Orleans who's falling in love with her twenty-one-year-old daughter's boyfriend. The woman is forty-two."

"A love triangle. What does the woman's husband think about it?"

"They're divorced. The lady says that the young man—he's thirty—is interested in her, too."

"The plot thickens," Whit said with a rakish grin. "What advice did Maudie give her?"

"Maudie said that the woman should ask herself who is more important to her, her daughter or the young man, because she's bound to lose one of them, depending on her priorities."

"True." Whit shook his head. "And I thought *I* had problems."

Emmy turned sideways to look at him. "What problems do you have?"

He glanced at her, then looked straight ahead again. "See any empty parking spaces? Right now that's my main problem."

His obvious dodge intrigued her. Was Whittier Hayes a man of mystery? Emmy wondered as she scanned the crowded streets and full parking lots. He gave the impression of being an open book, but there seemed to be a few pages missing.

"There!" Emmy pointed to the left. "That green car is pulling out."

"Right." Whit glanced in his mirrors before gunning for

the vacant slot. Horns honked behind them, but Whit
paid them no heed as he deftly parked. "Mission accomplished." He unfastened his seat belt and wasted no time
in getting out of the car and coming around the other side
to open Emmy's door. He locked the car, stuffed the keys
in his back pocket and stretched his arms above his head.
"Freedom!"

Emmy laughed and fitted her wide-brimmed straw hat
onto her head. "It's a perfect day for sight-seeing," she
said, feeling the light touch of the spring sun.

"I suggest we scout the area for a good restaurant." He
smiled, shoved his hands into his pockets and angled out
one elbow in an invitation.

Emmy linked her arm in his and fell into step beside
him as he made his way across the street and toward the
heart of Helen. The architecture was Swiss, with peaked
roofs and colorfully stenciled decorations. Helen was
surrounded by tall trees and blue sky, and the festive
atmosphere was contagious. A clown attracted a small
crowd of onlookers as he twisted long balloons into the
shapes of dogs, cats, elephants and horses, and farther
down the block another clown's juggling act drew applause.

Helen consisted of businesses with tourists in mind.
Candlemakers, basket weavers and glassblowers shared
the space with candy shops, bakeries and restaurants.
The jewelry shops and clothing stores carried more
souvenir items than practical ones, and nearly every store
sold picture postcards and maps of the business district.
The air was rich with the mouth-watering aromas of
freshly baked pastries, homemade fudge and spicy Polish
sausages.

Whit smacked his lips and stopped outside the fudge
factory, his gaze moving hungrily over the array of

sweets. "Let's have dessert first. This stuff looks so rich that all you have to do is look at it to make your teeth decay."

Emmy breathed in the smell of melting chocolate. "I don't care. I want some."

They went inside and bought a selection of white chocolate and almond bark, fudge and chocolate-covered pretzels, cherries and apricots, plus a couple of soft drinks with which to wash it all down. Whit located a bench that faced the juggling clown, and Emmy sat down with him and tore open the box of chocolates.

"Which one will you taste first?" she asked, holding out the box to him.

"Hmmm." He examined the contents carefully before taking one of the white-chocolate-covered pretzels. "This looks interesting."

"I'm going to try one of the apricots. After this, we won't want any lunch."

"Speak for yourself." Whit took a bite of the sugary pretzel, and his eyes rolled heavenward. "Delicious." He drank some cola and looked around at the milling crowd. "When were you here last?"

"Oh, let me see . . ." Emmy swallowed the sweet morsel of chocolate and apricot. "I guess it was about four years ago. Jerry's parents were visiting, and we brought them here to soak up some local color."

Whit rested his arms along the back of the bench and pinned her with serious, searching brown eyes. "Is divorce as awful as everybody says it is?"

"Worse." Emmy sighed and settled back against the bench. "I've heard of amicable ones, but I don't know how they come about. All of a sudden your husband is an intimate stranger, and the security of being two, instead of one, is—poof!—gone." She shook her head when

Whit offered her another chocolate. "No, thanks. Those are too rich for my blood."

"Just take a bite of this pretzel," Whit urged, extending the treat and tempting her.

Emmy obliged and nodded her approval. "You're right. Those are fabulous."

"Have you recovered from the divorce?"

"Yes, I guess so." She shrugged her shoulders in a halfhearted gesture. "It's a long, drawn-out process, but I'm handling it."

"Good for you."

She glanced at him sharply, trying to read something in his expression. "Why haven't you married?"

"I'm surprised the writer of an advice-to-the-lovelorn column would ask such a question." His eyes widened, and he laughed. "I'm unlucky in love, I guess."

Emmy shook her head and popped her sticky forefinger into her mouth. "You're selective." She smiled, gave a helpless shrug and took another candy from the box. "So much for willpower."

"Let's walk off some of these calories." Whit stood up and offered his arm to her.

"Good idea," Emmy said, rising to her feet and linking her arm through his again. "I remember there was a glassblower here. Let's find him."

They wandered toward the shops, which were packed with browsers. Several window displays caught Emmy's attention, and she paused to admire the handiwork. One shop displayed several handmade quilts that reflected hours of painstaking stitching. They located the glass-blower, and Emmy couldn't resist buying a miniature carousel. Whit bought an intricately carved candle from the candlemaker.

A few hours later Emmy agreed to a light lunch at a

German restaurant. Her feet were aching, and her appetite had returned. They ordered marinated beef sandwiches and creamy cole slaw; then Whit ordered coffee and a slice of German chocolate cake to share for dessert.

As she sat beside one of the restaurant's bay windows that gave a view of the passersby, Emmy watched a young man in jeans and a football jersey flirt with a girl who couldn't have been any older than seventeen.

"Do you still have your football jersey?" Emmy asked, facing Whit again.

He blinked several times, as if startled by her train of thought. "I don't think so. Why?"

Emmy shrugged and nodded toward the window. "I saw a guy wearing one and it made me think of the jersey you wore in college."

"So, you *do* remember something about me. I was beginning to wonder if I had just melted into the woodwork as far as you were concerned back then."

"I remember you," Emmy protested, surprised that he thought she hadn't paid any attention to him. "You were one of the big men on campus. A girl would have had to be blind not to have noticed you."

He smiled and offered her a bite of the cake, which she accepted. "I thought that you were so much in love with Jerry that you were blind to every other man."

"In a way, I guess I was. When I fall in love, I fall hard, and it takes me a long time to climb out of it." She peeked at him through her lashes. "Have you seen Jerry recently?"

"No, I haven't." He offered her another bite of cake and grinned. "Trust me."

Emmy shook her head and laughed softly before she let him slip the fork between her lips. The cake was rich and moist, and she chewed slowly and admired Whit's rakish grin. "It's hard to trust a man who has a grin like yours," she admitted with another laugh. "You look downright ornery, Whittier Hayes."

"Me?" His brown eyes widened.

"You. I think you have a mean streak in you."

The smile slipped from his lips, and he looked down into his coffee cup to avoid her gaze. "No, I don't. I'm stubborn, and I tend to have a one-track mind at times, but I'm not mean." He leaned back in his chair and gazed out the window. "Did you know that there were several guys in college who had crushes on you?"

"On me?" It was Emmy's turn to show surprise. "You're kidding."

"No, I'm serious."

"You're the one who turned heads," Emmy insisted. "All my girlfriends were so envious of me getting to work on the yearbook staff with you. They fell all over themselves when you entered the room and—"

"What about you?" he cut in, but he still didn't look at her. "Did I ever turn your head?"

Emmy swallowed hard, remembering that day in the park when Whit had held her close to him and almost made her forget that she was Jerry's girl. "Did I ever turn yours?"

A grin flirted with one corner of his mouth. "I asked you first."

"I asked you last."

The grin overtook him, and he pushed his chair back from the table. "It's a standoff. Ready to go?"

"Yes." Emmy waited at the restaurant door for Whit to pay the check while she repeated the disturbing conversation in her mind. Whit was a hard man to back into a corner, she mused. Just when she thought she had him pinned down, he wiggled free and left her clutching at thin air. There was a sense of mystery about him, as if he were hiding something from her. But what?

It was twilight when they arrived at Emmy's apartment. Fumbling with the door key, Emmy glanced up into Whit's face and saw hope spring eternal.

"Would you like to come in? I could make a pot of coffee, or would you rather have a glass of wine?"

"Wine is fine." Whit took the key from her fingers and deftly inserted it into the lock. "Don't have a nervous breakdown now, Emmy. You're almost home free."

Her high-pitched laugh revealed the sorry state of her nerves, and Emmy cut it off short. She entered the apartment and switched on the lamp beside the door. She had been completely at ease with Whit all day, so why was she a jumble of nerve endings now? she wondered. She took a deep breath and turned to face him. He was looking around the apartment, taking in the decor as he rocked back and forth on the balls of his feet.

"What do you think?" Emmy asked, desperate to break through the tension.

"Nice. Very nice." Whit smiled and tossed her keys onto an end table. "Do you miss your house?"

"Not in the least," Emmy said, tossing her hat and purse into a nearby chair on her way to the kitchen for the wine. "I'm trying to sell it. It's a case of a house owning me instead of me owning a house."

"I get the picture." Whit stood behind her as she selected a Burgundy from the wine rack, uncorked it and poured ample amounts into two crystal goblets. "I took the homeowner's plunge three years ago."

"Any regrets?"

"None. I'd had it up to here with apartment living." Whit drew his forefinger across his throat. "It seemed that no matter what apartment complex I lived in, I always had a neighbor who insisted on playing his stereo at maximum volume and threw wild parties every Friday and Saturday night."

"I don't have that problem yet, but I do have a wimpy little guy across the hall who wants to date me. He's harmless, but annoying." Emmy handed him one of the goblets. "Let's go into the living room."

"Okay." Whit stepped back and motioned for her to precede him.

Emmy sat on the sofa and felt her nerves flutter when Whit sat beside her. She wedged herself against the arm and twisted sideways to face him. His gentle smile told her that he had read and interpreted her body language.

"I don't know why I'm so edgy," Emmy said, abandoning her attempt at being subtle. "This is the part of dating I hate."

"That's funny," Whit said in a soft, sensual tone as he took one of her hands in his. "This is the part of dating I love." His thumb moved across the back of her hand before his fingers threaded between hers.

"Whit . . . I—uh—I'm not ready for this," Emmy stuttered, feeling her throat tighten. "I like being with you, but I'm not ready to be *with* you." She winced when he laughed under his breath. "Don't laugh at me."

"I'm sorry, but I think you're jumping way ahead of me." His eyes smoldered as he brought her hand to his lips. "I haven't asked you to sleep with me—yet."

"I know." Emmy gently extracted her hand from his. "I thought I read it in your expression."

"You probably did, but until I voice my thoughts they don't count."

Emmy stood up, unable to withstand the sexual tension that was closing in on her. She took a long drink of her wine and crossed the room to stand by the windows. Looking at the night sky calmed her and helped her put things into perspective. This jittery feeling was normal, she told herself. It was the thrill of the chase. It had been a while since she had been stalked by an expert hunter like—

Emmy tensed as Whit's arms came around her waist and his lips grazed her cheek, bringing a tide of warm color to her face.

"Trust me, Emmy," he whispered in her ear. "Don't be afraid of me. You set the rules, and I'll play by them. You can't blame me for wanting to make love to you."

Emmy rested the back of her head on his shoulder. "Right now that would be like jumping from the frying pan into the fire."

"I understand." He nuzzled her neck, and his arms tightened around her waist. The long muscles in his thighs flexed, making Emmy aware of the lean, hard length of him pressing against her. She released a shaky sigh when Whit took the glass of wine from her hand and set it on the coffee table.

"It's getting late," she said, and her whispery voice sounded weak and unsure. "I guess you'd better—"

He didn't let her finish her lame mutterings. His hands framed her face and tipped it up, and his mouth melted over hers. Longing corkscrewed in her stomach, and Emmy closed her eyes in surrender. She placed her hands over his and let him move her head this way and that as his mouth continued to rob her of her good sense. The tip of her tongue gathered the taste of wine from his lips, and he smiled against her mouth before drawing away.

His eyes glimmered with a deep amber light and seemed to devour her every feature, from her azure eyes

77

to the curling tumble of her dark hair. Emmy guided his hands from her face to her waist, then wrapped her arms around his neck and brought her lips up to his again. She inched her body up along his until she was standing on her tiptoes. His lips moved gently against hers, robbing and plundering until she was trembling with a searing desire she hadn't felt for years. Emmy flung back her head to gather air into her burning lungs, and Whit's mouth flamed up and down her throat while his hands moved up to the sides of her breasts. His thumbs skimmed across her nipples, drawing them into tight, tingling buds and making Emmy gasp softly. She drove her fingers through his hair and rained frantic kisses across his forehead, eyelids and the bridge of his nose as passion consumed her.

"Whit, oh, Whit . . ." She chanted his name between kisses, unleashing her desire and letting it rage through her untethered. Whit caught fire, and his mouth seared hers. His breath was hot and moist against her skin. Each kiss fanned the shooting flames within Emmy, melting her earlier resolve to go at a slow pace and with common sense.

The sheer power of her desire slammed through her, jolting her from her wild, mindless behavior. Her eyes popped open, and she stumbled backward just as Whit's fingers released the top button of her blouse. He looked at his hands, now in midair and unbuttoning nothing, then lifted his gaze wonderingly to hers.

"Was it something I didn't say?" he asked, letting his hands drop to his sides.

Emmy ran a hand through her hair, lifting it from her forehead and pushing it back from her flushed face. "I'm doing just what I said I wouldn't do," she explained shakily. "I'm jumping into the fire, and I can't do that, Whit. I can't."

He shrugged and fingered his square jawline. "It was just a good-night kiss, Emmy."

"Just a good-ni—" She smiled when she saw the teasing glint in his eyes. "You're absolutely right. It was just a good-night kiss, and not a very good one at that."

"Oh?" He crossed his arms against his chest. "On a scale of one to ten . . ."

"Twelve," Emmy said with a laugh as she moved past him to the door. "And you know it." She opened the door and turned back to him. Her nerves fluttered when he stood his ground for a few moments before giving a little shrug and moving toward her.

"I know when I've overstayed my welcome." Whit stopped in front of her and curled his fingers under chin to make her meet his steady gaze. "Thanks for a wonderful Saturday. On a scale of one to ten it was a twelve."

"I'm glad." She accepted his brief parting kiss.

"What are you doing tomorrow?"

"Housework and laundry." She laughed and gave him a gentle push across the threshold. "Call me Monday."

He propped one arm against the doorframe and leaned into her territory again. "I'll call you tomorrow."

"No, don't." She laughed and started to close the door.

"Maybe we can get together for brunch."

"No, we can't."

"You're the best kisser I've ever known, Maude Edith Bakersfield."

Still laughing, Emmy closed the door, then leaned back against it and listened to the pounding of her heart in her ears and the retreating sound of Whit's footsteps in the hallway. She shut her eyes and rested one hand over her racing heart. Laughter bubbled through her, making her feel light-headed and carefree.

Minutes passed before she pushed herself away from the door and walked across the living room to her bedroom. While she showered she thought of Whit and the way he moved her—the way he moved through her like a hot, restless wind. Whit was a force to be reckoned with, she mused, and she wasn't at all sure she could harness the passion he aroused inside her. It was like trying to hold on to the tail of a tornado.

After emerging from the shower, she slipped into a robe and flung herself across her four-poster bed. The night-light cast a rosy glow in the room, matching the one she felt inside as she relived little, important moments of the day: Whit's arm draped across her shoulders as they strolled through Helen; Whit feeding her bites of chocolate cake and candy; Whit asking her to help him select a candle to buy. Whit, Whit, Whit.

Emmy hugged herself as her emotions swelled to almost painful proportions. Was she falling in love? If so, it was too fast and too furious to last long. She was right to rein in her feelings and take it slower, even though her sensual self had been eager for fulfillment. Longing curled through her, and she languished in it. It had been so long since she had given herself up to the sheer luxury of chemical and physical attraction, and it was heaven to experience it again, and to know that the feelings were mutual.

She hadn't realized until this evening that there was a barren spot in her life, but Whit had made her aware of it when he kissed her. Suddenly the void had widened, and she had ached to have him fill it. She needed romance in her life, Emmy told herself firmly. One failed romance wasn't the end of the world. Maudie would be the first to tell someone in Emmy's place to dust herself off and start all over again. What had Whit said about love? She thought for a few moments before she remembered.

"The only abnormality is the incapacity to love," Emmy repeated with a dreamy smile. What a man! Her smile grew cunning, and a delicious thrill raced through her. The chase was on, and she knew it was only a matter of time before the hunter captured her.

5

Dear T.C.,

Congratulations on your success with Susie. Take it easy from here on in. Romance is the operative word and the way to any woman's heart.

Fools rush in where angels fear to tread, so be an angel and woo Susie with hearts and flowers, and not with a sudden confession of your love for her. You've known of your feelings for years, but this will be news to Susie, and I doubt if she's ready to hear it—or if she will believe it in this early stage of your reunion.

Let me know how your date goes, and remember that romance can go a long way. Roses are a good beginning. Breathes there a woman with soul so dead who never to herself hath said, "I wish he'd be romantic and send me a dozen roses"?

Maudie

Emmy glanced at her watch as she entered the building that housed her lawyer's office. She was a few minutes early for her appointment, so she went to the restaurant on the lobby level and sat down at one of the small tables to enjoy a cup of hot coffee and collect her thoughts before the meeting with the lawyers and Jerry.

Mondays were usually the worst day of the week for her, but this Monday was different. She smiled as the sweet memories of her Saturday with Whit wrapped around her. She'd almost floated into the office this morning, and Bertha had been quick to notice her sunny disposition, she recalled as she sipped the coffee while her memory replayed the earlier conversation for her own amusement.

"You must have had a terrific weekend," Bertha had said, obviously fishing for all the juicy details.

Emmy had grinned and hummed a happy tune while she worked on one of her columns.

"Well, what happened?" Bertha had demanded after a long, expectant silence.

Not wanting to share her intimate feelings, Emmy had given a little shrug as she glanced out the window. "Isn't it a beautiful morning?"

"Are you going to tell me about your weekend or not?"

"I'm not." Emmy had softened her refusal with another bright smile. "I'm taking a long lunch hour today."

"Oh?" Bertha had wiggled her eyebrows. "Is it business or pleasure?"

"Neither. It's Jerry." Emmy had laughed at Bertha's sour frown. "Don't worry, Bert. Not even Jerry can spoil this gorgeous day for me. I'm supposed to meet with his lawyers and mine over the lunch hour to iron out the details on the house."

"I hope things work out for you on that score." Bertha had laughed with a shake of her head as she tore open another envelope. "Whatever happened over the weekend must have been pretty special."

"On a scale of one to ten, it was a twelve," Emmy had said, laughing at her private joke before turning back to the word processor and addressing herself to the trials and tribulations of people she knew only as "Dumped in Dallas," "Ruined Romeo" and "Torch Carrier."

Now Emmy finished her coffee and tossed the plastic cup into a nearby wastebasket. She went to the bank of elevators and waited for one to descend to her level. The doors hissed open, and Emmy stepped in, then was whisked up to the seventh floor. She glanced in the mirrored panels to check her hair and makeup before she left the compartment and walked briskly to the correct office.

Feeling confident and contented, she entered the lawyer's office and surprised Jerry by greeting him with a cordial "hello" and a saucy grin. She told herself that nothing could dampen her high spirits, but two hours later she stormed from her lawyer's office, trying in vain to hold onto a shred of her previous good mood.

"Hey, wait up, Emmy!"

Emmy whirled to face Jerry. "What is it? I've got to get back to the office."

Jerry caught up with her and ran a hand through his thinning blond hair. "Don't go away mad, Emmy. I'm just fighting for what's mine. You can't blame me for that."

"I certainly can, and I do!"

"You're being selfish again," Jerry charged, fixing a

superior expression on his narrow face. "You're about to rake in tons of money on your book. You're in the catbird seat and I'm—"

"Making a nuisance of yourself, as usual," Emmy interrupted, refusing to give an inch. "The judge has agreed to hear your appeal so I'll see you in court—again."

"I deserve half of what we get for the house and you know it."

"All I know is that I'll be glad when you give up and leave me alone." She gave him a cold glare. "If you have anything else to say, say it to my lawyer." Turning on her heel, she started for the elevator again.

"I heard that you're seeing a friend of mine," Jerry called, then grinned when she stopped and turned to face him. "Whit Hayes, right?"

Wariness stole through her as she examined the vicious glint in Jerry's hazel eyes. She cautioned herself to remain calm. Jerry was probably repeating gossip he'd heard through the grapevine, but she didn't like his smug smile. Had he talked with Whit over the weekend?

"Whit is handling the publicity for my book," Emmy said, carefully selecting her words. "ACTION hired his firm."

Jerry sauntered past her and punched the down arrow for the elevator. "I know." He leaned a shoulder against the wall and adopted a cocky pose. "I like Whit. He's a good man, and you need one right now."

Emmy stiffened and looked away from him. He was playing a game with her, she told herself, and she wouldn't play by his rules.

"No doubt about it," Jerry continued. "You need a level-headed man to guide your career. Whit will steer you in the right direction."

The elevator reached their level, and the doors opened. Emmy nodded toward it.

"Go on, Jerry. I'll take the next one."

"Don't be childish, Emmy. Can't we behave as two adults and—"

"Jerry, don't push your luck," Emmy said between clenched teeth. "Go while the going is good."

Giving a careless shrug, Jerry stepped into the elevator. "Okay, okay." His gaze moved from the toes of her brown leather pumps to the crown of her head, and a lazy smile graced his lips. "You're looking good, Emmy. Real good."

The doors slid shut, and Emmy breathed a sigh of disgust as she hit the button on the panel again. What a creep! A chill passed through her, followed by an odd sense of sorrow. Why did it have to disintegrate to this sorry state? she wondered as she waited for the elevator. Jerry was a stranger to her, a hateful, bitter stranger. What had become of the man she had married, the man who had made her laugh and love? They had become snipers, taking potshots at each other.

Emmy stepped into the elevator, feeling tired and defeated. She didn't want to hate Jerry, but he seemed to push her in that direction.

And what of Whit? Had Jerry spoken to Whit, or was he merely using the other man as ammunition?

After leaving the building, Emmy walked in the direction of her own office as her thoughts and feelings clashed. Jerry's remark about Whit managing her career haunted her. One thing she didn't need was another man trying to think for her.

Reaching her office, Emmy directed a halfhearted smile in Bertha's direction and knew that her assistant could tell that things hadn't gone well during the meeting.

"Where's that sunny smile you had when you left here?" Bertha asked as Emmy deposited her purse on her desk.

"I left it back at the lawyer's office." Emmy touched a long gold box on her desk. "What's this?"

"It arrived for you about an hour ago. Looks like flowers. Maybe they'll bring that smile back."

"I doubt it." Emmy untied the red bow. "The judge has decided to hear Jerry's appeal."

"I'm sorry, hon," Bertha said, her voice dipping with sincerity. "What is it?"

Emmy slammed the lid back on the box. "Roses!" She backed away as if the box contained a dozen snakes instead of a dozen American Beauties. "That's all I need!"

"Oh, dear, you're allergic to roses, aren't you?" Bertha asked as she stood up and hurried toward Emmy's desk. "I'll take them away."

"Yes, and hurry!" Emmy placed a finger under her nose, already feeling a tickling and knowing that a series of sneezes was building up. "What does the card say?"

Bertha carried the box to the other side of the room before she opened it again and withdrew the white card. She placed it on her desk. "You read it while I take these away. I'll give them to the accountant's secretary next door."

"Good idea." Emmy waited until Bertha had left the office before she moved forward and picked up the card.

Roses are red, violets are blue. Don't forget the newspaper interview tomorrow I set up for you.

Love,
Whit

Newspaper interview? Emmy went to her desk and checked her calendar, but there was no mention of the appointment.

"She was thrilled," Bertha said, entering the office again. "Who sent them?"

"Whit Hayes." Emmy looked up from the calendar on her desk. "The card said something about a newspaper interview, but I don't remember . . ."

"Oh, right!" Bertha bustled over to Emmy's desk and picked up a pink slip of paper. "Whit called right after you left and said he'd set up an interview for you with a reporter from one of the local papers. I jotted down the information."

Emmy took the slip of paper from Bertha. "I wish he'd checked with me first before he set this up."

"Is there a problem?"

"No, but he should have talked to me about it before he made the appointment. It's common business courtesy. He's working for me. I'm not working for him."

Bertha's brows lifted in surprise. "He's just doing his job."

Emmy collapsed in the chair and sighed. "I know, but I don't like the way he's doing it. I don't need another man pulling my strings."

Bertha gave her a measured stare. "Why don't you take the rest of the day off? I think that meeting at the lawyer's has upset you and—"

"No, I want to work." Emmy swiveled her chair to face the computer screen. "I'm okay." She forced a smile to her lips. "Really, Bert, I'm fine. Let's get back to work."

"Okay." Bertha shrugged and went back to her desk and the mail that waited.

Maybe she was overreacting, Emmy thought, but it was better to get things straight before they got out of hand. At the first opportunity she would tell Whit that he was to consult her before he made appointments. In fact, it probably wouldn't hurt if she kept a cautious tongue in her head around him and a lock on her heart. Combining business with pleasure had never been a successful recipe for her. Hadn't she vowed to keep her business separate from her private life after her divorce? That had seemed the only answer at the time, but Whit had made her break her promise.

Emmy turned her chair around until her back was to Bertha. She stared out the window at the reflection of the sun in the glass buildings as her niggling worries grew into winged monsters. When she'd given Jerry an inch, he'd taken a mile. Why should Whit be any different? If she was putty in his hands, he'd try to mold her and her career, and she didn't want that to happen. She wanted to be captain of her own ship, and the sooner Whit realized that the better.

Whit whistled a merry tune as he pressed the bell and waited for Emmy to answer the door. He held up the bottle of wine, examined the label again, then shifted the box of roses to the crook of his other arm. He rang the bell again, then glanced at his watch. Maybe she hadn't come home from the office yet. It was just a few minutes after five.

He set the bottle of wine and the box of roses outside the door, then leaned back against the wall, crossed his ankles and arms and smiled. Courting was fun, he decided. Usually he was too impatient to waste time on such trivial pursuits, but this wasn't half-bad. It was like having the bases loaded and waiting for the next Atlanta

Brave batter to either hit a homer or bite the dust. The tension would build and build until suddenly the air quivered with the sound of a bat cracking into a white blur and arcing it into the bleachers. Of course this tension was different, and there was more at stake than just another game won or lost. He glanced at the gifts he'd placed outside Emmy's door and grinned.

The last time he'd bought roses for a woman had been a year ago for his mother on her thirty-fifth wedding anniversary, and the last time he'd bought a bottle of wine for a woman had been to smooth his way into a flight attendant's hotel room a few months ago. What was her name? Betty? Barbara? Something starting with a *B*.

Whit laughed under his breath. The only name he could remember clearly was Emmy's. All those other names of the women he had known had faded into never-never land the moment he had kissed Emmy and felt that old, simmering passion burst into life again.

He settled more comfortably against the wall and closed his eyes as a distant memory wafted to him from the far reaches of his mind. The details of that day long ago eluded him, but he could see Emmy in white shorts and a red and white striped shirt as she sat on a park swing and instructed him to push her higher and higher. Her laughter, like her voice, had been husky and alluring. He had enjoyed pushing her in the swing at first, but it had soon become an intolerable torture. Finally he could stand it no longer, and he had wrapped his arms tightly about her waist to keep her suspended. Her feet had dangled inches from the ground, and she had looked over her shoulder at him in a questioning way.

He had felt as if he had not only stopped Emmy's

forward progress, but time's as well. Never in his life had he wanted to kiss a woman so desperately. Her lips had been a mere inch from his, and he could remember how soft and moist they had looked that day, and how he had wanted to break all the barriers between them and drink his fill of her. But in the end he had let her go and made fast tracks in the opposite direction.

God, what was it about her that made him writhe with longing? How had she managed to weave herself so tightly into his soul and not even be aware of it? Was she so blind that she had not known that he had fallen head over heels in love with her back in college?

A "ding" sounded in the corridor, and Whit opened his eyes and pushed himself away from the wall as the elevator opened and Emmy stepped out. She looked delicious in a cream skirt and blazer and a chocolate brown shirt. A startled expression raced across her face when she saw him.

"What are you doing here?" she asked as she approached him, keys in hand.

Whit bent over and retrieved the wine and roses, then straightened and held them out to her. "I'm making a special delivery to a special lady."

She glanced at the wine, then narrowed her eyes when she looked at the long box. "I hope those aren't roses."

Her oddly phrased question dented his good tidings, and he frowned. "Yes, they are. Just like the ones I sent to your office. You got them, didn't you?" Whit's brows met in a scowl.. "Why are you backing away from me."

"Those . . . those roses." She covered her nose and mouth with one hand. "Don't open the box. Keep them away from me."

"Why? What's wrong?"

"I'm allergic to them. The mere mention of them sends me into sneezing . . ." She sneezed and plastered herself against the opposite wall. "Sneezing fits."

Frustration exploded in him. "Well, why the hell didn't you tell me that before?" He put the box behind his back, but she held her ground.

"You didn't ask me before!" Emmy motioned him to one side. "Let me get the door."

He moved aside as she unlocked her apartment. "Can I come in and share this wine with you? Or are you allergic to wine, too?"

"No, I'm not."

"Good." He started forward, but Emmy placed a hand against his chest and checked his progress. "Now what? I'll leave the roses out here."

She turned pleading eyes up to him. "Whit, it's been a long day. I'm not in the mood for company."

"I won't stay long."

"I've made other plans for the evening. Sorry." Her hand dropped from his shirtfront. "Thank you for your thoughtfulness, but you should have called first to see if I was free for the evening."

Whit put a lid on his temper. "Forgive me." He reached for her hand and placed the bottle of wine in it. "Is it my imagination, or is there an arctic wind blowing through this corridor?"

His acid humor provoked another frown of irritation from her.

"Not that you need reminding, but ours is a business relationship, and I've discovered from experience that mixing business with pleasure is dynamite."

Her statement rattled him, and he shook his head, trying to force his thoughts into coherency. "Hold on a minute. What was Saturday? Was that a business meeting?"

"Saturday was just . . . just a couple of old college friends getting together for a little reminiscing—"

"And a little romancing," he interrupted curtly. "Or have you forgotten those good-night kisses which you rated so highly? What brought on this loss of memory?"

Emmy sighed and stepped back from him, putting the threshold between them. "I don't like the way you set up that newspaper interview without consulting me first."

"But I—"

"From now on I'd appreciate it if you'd let me have the final say on all appointments. This is my book and my business, not yours."

Whit ran a hand through his hair, not caring if he mussed it. "Let me get this straight. You're mad because I set up an appointment for you. You're mad because I'm doing what I'm being paid to do. Is that about it?"

"I'm not mad; I'm just trying to make myself clear on this point. I might have made other plans for tomorrow and been unavailable for the interview. I'm not at your beck and call."

"Bertha checked your calendar and told me it was clear."

"She did?" Surprise registered in her eyes.

"She did." He narrowed his eyes and stared her down.

She looked at the bottle of wine and took a deep breath. "You should have asked me, not Bertha."

"You weren't in the office when I called."

"Then you should have called back later and spoken to me!" Her voice rose fractionally, and she blushed. "Look, thanks for the wine and the"—she glanced at the box—"and for those. I'll be at the interview tomorrow, but from now on—"

"I've got my orders." He saluted her, then wished he hadn't resorted to sarcasm when her eyes grew cold. "We leave for Miami Wednesday."

"Yes, I know."

He didn't want to leave while she was still cool and remote. "Emmy, I'm sorry. I should have called and all that, but just because I didn't is no reason to relegate me to the status of just another business associate. We're more to each other than that, aren't we?"

She hesitated a few moments before answering in a barely discernible whisper, "Yes, I guess so."

"I'll meet you at the newspaper tomorrow and—"

"That's not necessary," she cut in.

"It's part of my job. *Business.*" He emphasized the last word, angry that she wouldn't relent. "I'll meet you there."

"Okay." She took another step backward. "See you tomorrow."

The door closed in his face, and Whit barely kept himself from giving it a hard kick. What had gotten into her? She was making a federal case over nothing!

Tucking the box of flowers under this arm, he strode toward the elevator and swore under his breath. The doors opened, and a middle-aged woman gave him a worried glance as he took his place beside her. She edged away, and Whit realized that his expression must border on murderous. He glanced at the box under his arm and forced a tense smile to his lips.

"Do you have anything against roses?"

"W—what?" The woman placed a hand over her heart, and her dark eyes looked huge behind her bifocals. "I . . . roses? No. I like them."

"Good." He held out the box to her. "Here's a dozen. You can have them." The doors opened, and when the woman made no move to take the box from him, Whit pushed them into her arms.

"Why are you giving them to me?"

"I always give roses to women who ride in elevators with me." Whit grinned at her baffled expression. "It's something my mother taught me." He gave a short wave and escaped the woman's sputtering attempts at thanking him.

After leaving the building, Whit folded himself behind the wheel of his car and merged with the teeming traffic as his thoughts returned to Emmy's change of heart. What could have prompted such a—

Whit slammed one hand on the steering wheel. Jerry! He'd run into Jerry last Friday and told him he was working with Emmy. Could Jerry have said something to Emmy to make her distrust him? Damn! Whit gripped the wheel and ground his teeth together in frustration.

Jerry Jennings was keeping him from Emmy again. Just like old times.

A moan worked up his throat, and he steered the car in the direction of the gym where he had a membership. He'd work off his frustration and then he could think clearly. He was probably jumping to conclusions. Emmy had just had a bad day and took it out on him. Tomorrow would be different. She'd be herself again, and they could get back to that wonderfully encouraging place they'd been Saturday. The next days would be crucial, but at least he wouldn't have to worry about Jerry feeding lies to Emmy. He'd have Emmy to himself in Miami, and he'd take advantage of that.

He grinned and felt his spirits lift as he parked the car in the gym lot. Time was still on his side. Nothing to worry about, he thought, giving himself a mental pep talk. Shouldn't let this little setback get you down. Tomorrow is another day, and then there's Miami to look forward to. He started whistling again as he left the car and walked to the gym.

Emmy tied the belt of her robe at her waist as she made her way from her bedroom to the kitchen for a glass of milk before she retired for the evening. Her gaze fell on the bottle of wine sitting on the kitchen cabinet, and she winced before picking it up and placing it in her wine rack.

She hadn't handled the earlier confrontation with Whit very well, she thought as she poured herself a glass of milk and took it into the living room. Curling up in her favorite easy chair, she drank the milk and dropped into a thoughtful mood.

Whit was always catching her off-guard. He'd been the last person she'd expected to find standing in front of her door when she arrived home this afternoon, and she hadn't had time to fully examine what she would say to him about making the appointment without consulting her first. She'd been ungracious and irrational, throwing his gifts back in his face and sputtering gibberish about mixing business with pleasure. He must think she was a basket case.

It was so easy for her to give advice to others—to strangers—but it was so difficult to handle her own sticky situations. The terrible part of this whole mess was that she wanted a personal relationship with Whit. Had he believed her when she'd said she just wanted a business relationship? She hadn't convinced herself, so it was doubtful that she had convinced him.

Emmy threw back her head and groaned her frustration. Everything was so complicated! Why did Whit have to be Jerry's old buddy? It would be so much simpler if she hadn't known him years ago, if she hadn't been introduced to him through Jerry and if Whit hadn't kept up his friendship with Jerry after college. It was foolish of her to be wary of anything or anyone Jerry Jennings had dealings with, but she couldn't help it. And that crack Jerry had made about Whit handling her career hadn't helped matters.

She finished her milk, rinsed out the glass and went back into the bedroom. Pulling the draperies back, she stared at the sparkling Atlanta lights and felt loneliness descend over her. She tried to shake it off, but it persisted. Blast Whit Hayes for bringing these feelings back into her life! She had finally adjusted to being single, and suddenly she was longing to be part of someone else's life. She wanted to be appreciated as a woman again, and, more importantly, she wanted to be loved again as only a special man could love her.

With a harsh sigh she turned from the window and removed her robe before climbing into bed. The sheets felt cold and empty, and she turned her face into the pillow and fought back a sudden urge to cry.

6

Dear Maudie,

Disaster! My date with Susie went wonderfully—or
so I thought. I followed up with flowers as you
instructed and she threw them in my face! For the life
of me, I don't understand what she's so upset about!
When I left her after the date she was in the palm of
my hand, but when I gave her the flowers she wanted
to apply the palm of her hand to the side of my face.

If I live to be 100 I'll never understand women.
Please help me, Maudie. What do I do now? Susie is
still speaking to me, but she's cool and distant. Is it
possible that someone is telling tales about me behind
my back? I'm waiting for your advice and hoping you
can unravel the mystery of women for me.

Torch Carrier

"What do you make of that?" Bertha asked. Her raspy voice floated easily across the phone lines from Atlanta to Miami.

Emmy frowned and shook her head, then realized that Bertha couldn't see her. "I'm thinking. This has me stumped."

"Join the club. Poor Torch Carrier! He must be bouncing off the walls. What's with this Susie character?"

"I don't know, but something is rotten in Denmark."

"Atlanta," Bertha corrected. "The postmark is from Atlanta. You've got to help Torch Carrier, since he's one of our own."

"Yes, you're right, but I've got to give this a little thought. Maybe T.C. is leaving out part of the story. It just doesn't make sense that Susie would throw a bouquet back in his face if the date had gone as well as he indicated. I'll get back to you later this evening with an answer to his letter. We can't keep him waiting."

"Right," Bertha agreed. "Especially since his story is being followed by so many people. I've had several letters this week from people who are rooting for him and Susie."

"Tag this letter with an 'urgent' marker so that it and the answer will be published no later than the first of next week."

"Will do." Bertha was quiet for a moment, as if making a notation of Emmy's order. "Well, how's Miami? How did the autograph party go? Was it as successful as the one you had here?"

"More successful. We ran out of books! I couldn't believe it. I have an interview at a television station today, and then I'm coming home. Our flight leaves tomorrow afternoon, but I'll still call you today about T.C.'s problem."

"Good. I've missed you, and I'll sure be glad to have you back."

"I'll only be back for two days, then we're flying to New Orleans."

Bertha groaned into the telephone, making Emmy laugh. "Go ahead and laugh! You're having fun in the sun while I'm toiling away in this office."

"Who's having fun in the sun?" Emmy sighed and looked out the window of her hotel suite at the stretch of golden sand. The sun was dipping below the horizon, painting the sky with indigo and orange. "I haven't even walked on the beach yet. Whit is a slave driver."

"How are things between you two, or are you still keeping all that to yourself?"

"We're on friendly terms." Emmy picked up the telephone and moved closer to the window. Her gaze followed a couple strolling along the beach. "Bertha, do you think it's possible for two people to juggle an emotional and professional relationship?"

"It depends on the two people and how important they are to each other."

"Jerry and I botched it."

"Yes, but Jerry was never a genius at business. Don't go lumping Whit Hayes in with Jerry Jennings. As far as I can see, they're as different as night and day."

"Yes, you're right." Emmy shook off her blue mood and forced a brightness into her voice. "If that's all, I'll talk to you later tonight or by tomorrow morning on that Torch Carrier letter."

"Gotcha. For heaven's sake, get out there on the beach before you fly back here. You deserve it."

"I'll try. 'Bye, Bert."

"Bye-bye, hon."

Emmy replaced the receiver and turned her attention back to the setting sun and the beach. People were gathering their beach blankets and umbrellas and leaving, and Emmy envied them. It would be so nice to relax all day long in the sun, but Whit had kept her hopping ever since they had landed in Miami yesterday afternoon. By the time she had completed the autograph party and attended a reception last night, she had been exhausted. She had slept late and indulged in a huge breakfast in bed, then dressed for a newspaper interview that Whit had set up. The interview had taken two hours, but Whit had complimented her on her handling of it. He'd assured her that she was getting the hang of it.

It was easier than she had thought. The autograph parties were fun, because she met so many people and accepted their praise of her column. The interviews were more stressful, but even so, she had enjoyed them for the most part. The reporters had all seemed genuinely interested in her work and her success at it. Whit had kept his word and faithfully consulted her before making any appointments. More than once, Emmy had tried to find some way to make amends for her ill manners that day he had surprised her with wine and roses. For some reason she couldn't seem to break through his cool, remote facade. He wasn't ready to accept a truce.

A knock on the door pulled her from her musings, and Emmy started across the spacious room to answer it.

"Who is it?"

"Whit."

Emmy glanced down at her blue terry cloth shorts and matching top, shrugged and opened the door. "Hello. I hope you haven't set up another interview because I just threw on these clothes and it will take me at least an hour to—"

"No more interviews until tomorrow, as planned," Whit broke in with a slight chuckle. "Can I come in?"

"Sure." Emmy backed up and let him enter. "I just got off the phone with Bertha. She misses me."

"Doesn't she like holding down the fort all by herself?"

"I guess not." Emmy let her gaze wander over his casual jeans and white pullover shirt. It had been days since she'd seen him in anything other than a suit and tie. "I have a couple of sodas in the refrigerator, or would you rather have a beer?"

"A soda would hit the spot. Thanks." He settled his tall, lean frame in one of the chairs by the window.

Emmy got the two cans of soda and took her time in opening them and pouring the contents into two glasses. She studied Whit while she prepared the refreshments, thinking how attractive he looked with the last fingers of sunlight outlining his profile. The beginnings of tomorrow's beard shadowed the lower half of his face, and she longed to run her fingertips along the roughness of his jawline.

"I've stopped by to give you a few pointers on how to handle tomorrow's interview," he said, turning his head to look at her. "The talk show host is—"

"Why do I need pointers? Only this afternoon you told me I was getting the hang of it." Emmy handed him one of the glasses and sat in the chair on the other side of the lamp table. "I can handle it."

Whit's brown eyes narrowed as he took a sip of cola, and his voice was deceptively soft when he spoke. "I hate to sound like a broken record, but I'm just doing my job. I've worked with this talk show host before, and I think it's important for you to know something about how he works before you go on his program. Of course, if you'd rather go in cold, that's your business."

Emmy glanced out the window and mentally bit her tongue. Why did she allow herself to cut him off at the knees every chance she got? She wanted to regain his affection, and this wasn't the way to do it. Looking at him again, she offered a smile of apology.

"I'm sorry, Whit. Go ahead with what you were saying."

"Thank you."

Emmy frowned at his stiff, uncharacteristic response, but made no comment on it.

"As I was saying, the host of the talk show is a ham and has an annoying habit of talking more than his guests. He'll ask a question, but before you can fully answer it, he'll break in with some story about himself. When he says something like, 'That reminds me of the time . . .' or 'That's interesting, but let me tell you about the time . . .' you gracefully cut him off and finish your answer."

"How does one *gracefully* do that?" Emmy asked.

The corner of his mouth rose in that irresistible lopsided grin. "You kick him in the shin." He laughed at her shocked expression. "Seriously, you just give him a taste of his own medicine and counter with 'And that reminds me of the letter included in my book about the woman who could never get a word in edgewise around her husband. My advice to her was to interrupt him as often as he interrupts her and see how he likes it.'" Whit shrugged. "Something along those lines."

Emmy sipped her cola slowly and eyed Whit with growing admiration. He really was something, she thought. He knew his business, making her fully aware of how much she could learn from him.

Sensing her intent regard, Whit arched his brows and leaned forward a bit. "Something wrong? You're looking at me as if you're ready to pounce."

Emmy laughed and felt warm color stain her cheeks. If only he knew how often she had wanted to pounce on him lately. He was a cunning hunter, dropping back and making her anticipate when or if he would make his move.

"I was just overwhelmed by your expertise, that's all. I would never have thought of that tactic, but I can see how it could work beautifully and to my advantage. I have a lot to learn from you."

"And I have a lot to learn from you."

"Oh? Like what?"

He finished his cola and set the glass on the table. "Like what other things are you allergic to, besides roses?"

"Cauliflower and cabbage."

"Well, I don't think I'll be sending you a bouquet of those. I wish you'd told me about your allergy before I forked over mucho bucks for those roses."

"The subject never came up," Emmy reminded him. "It's not my custom to give a list of my allergies to every man I meet."

"You have a point." He lapsed into silence and stared moodily at his laced fingers. "Emmy, I ran into Jerry last week, at the Laundromat of all places. I told him I was working with you." His velvety brown gaze moved up to her face. "I didn't see anything wrong with telling him, but maybe I shouldn't have mentioned it."

A tiny alarm sounded in her mind. Did Whit think she was mad at him just because he had mentioned her name around Jerry? She leaned forward and placed a hand on his arm.

"If you hadn't told Jerry, I would have eventually. I know you haven't been gossiping to him about us."

"Good." His grin spread into his eyes, lightening them to the color of cinnamon. "Could I ask you something without your taking it the wrong way?"

"Ask."

"Did Jerry say something to you that made you want to throw water on our budding relationship?"

Emmy's fingers slid from his arm, and she sat back in her chair. "Sort of. Actually, he just reminded me of how exasperating it is when someone is trying to run your life for you. I don't want to be placed in that situation again and . . . well, when you made that appointment for me without asking first, I blew it all out of proportion. I thought that you might be getting a little too heavy-handed with my business."

"So you weren't disappointed in my courting procedures?"

Emmy laughed at his choice of words. "Courting procedures? Is that what you've been doing? Are you wooing me?"

Whit placed a hand over his heart and feigned a swoon, his brown eyes rolling up before his thick lashes concealed them. "You really know how to hurt a guy! Of course I've been wooing you. I don't buy two dozen roses and imported wine for every client!"

Emmy's laughter died as she thought of her conflicting needs. "I guess what bothers me is that I know what wooing leads to." She glanced at him and saw that he was watching her intently, as if reading her every thought. "I've had to make quite a few adjustments over the past few years, and I've just recently found a comfortable niche. I'm not at all sure it would be wise for me to become involved with anyone right now."

"Am I just anyone?"

"No, but my common sense tells me that—"

"We're already involved with each other, Emmy. Your common sense should tell you that, too." He laced his fingers behind his head and pinned her with a steady, no-nonsense gaze. "You can put a lid on our situation if you want, but eventually the lid is going to be blown off. I can guarantee it."

Emmy stood up, unable to confront his frankness. "I'm so restless. I was telling Bertha that I haven't even set foot on that beach out there, and it's driving me crazy." She paced aimlessly, finally coming to a halt in front of the windows again. "The sun has gone to bed."

"Why don't you and I take a walk along the beach?" Whit stood up and captured one of her hands, giving it a little tug. "I'm restless, too. It might have something to do with hearing the sound of the surf. Every time I'm near the ocean I feel as if I'm being tossed from one mood to another. It will be good for both of us to get away from this hotel and walk off our nerves."

"Let me grab a sweater or something and I'll be right with you." She extracted her hand from his and went into the bedroom. She removed her top and slipped on a white sweatshirt with long sleeves and a hood, then brushed her hair, added a swipe of mulberry lipstick to her full lips, and rejoined Whit in the sitting room.

He was at the door and motioned her to precede him. "Don't forget your room key."

"Oh, right." Emmy grabbed the key from off the table, tucked it into her pocket and left the room. "Have you lived in Atlanta all your life?" she asked as Whit fell into step with her.

"No. I was born in Salt Lake City, but we moved to Atlanta when I was ten. What about you?"

"Atlanta born and bred."

"A genuine Georgia peach, huh?" He stepped into the elevator with her and pushed the lobby button.

"I guess so. Do your parents still live in Atlanta?"

"They moved to Mobile a few years ago when my mother inherited the family farm there. My younger brother and his wife farm the property, and my parents are enjoying retired life."

"Good for them. Do you have any other brothers or sisters?"

"I have an older sister who lives in Jackson. She's a high school teacher, and her husband is the principal at an elementary school. What about you?"

"You're looking at a spoiled only child."

The elevator let them out into the lobby. Whit laughed and took one of her hands in his. "If I had you, I'd spoil you, too."

Her pulse pounded into life, and Emmy laughed at herself for reacting so strongly to his innocent statement, but she couldn't help indulging in a brief fantasy of how lovely it would be to be spoiled by Whittier Hayes. The beach stretched out before them, bereft of the sun-worshipers, and an ocean breeze raised goose-bumps on Emmy's bare legs. She glanced down at her lightly tanned thighs.

"I guess it's a sin to return from Florida without a golden tan," she mused aloud.

"There's sun in Atlanta, too." Whit released her hand and draped his arm across her shoulders, gently pulling her closer to his warmth. He tipped back his head and sighed. "Will you look at that sky? It looks as if you could reach up and touch the Milky Way." He lifted his other hand, and his fingertips groped for the feel of star fire.

Emmy looked up into his face and was instantly

transfixed. A breeze ruffled his hair a moment before his eyes met hers, making Emmy's heart leap into her throat. He lowered his extended hand, and his fingertips smoothed a path from her winged brow to the corner of her mouth. A gentle smile tugged at his own mouth, and his eyes enjoyed her, lingering on her lips and narrowing when she wet them with the tip of her tongue.

The push and pull of the ocean merged within Emmy, and when the surf moved out to the vastness beyond, Emmy moved into Whit's embrace. His mouth fell to hers and tugged until her lips parted in sweet submission. The surf rolled in again, and waves of desire washed over Emmy, drowning her in the experience. Whit's hands flattened against her back, then slipped lower to cradle her hips and pull her more tightly to him. Her pulse pounded for supremacy over the roar of the surf and won, making Emmy aware only of the man who seemed to enfold her in a sea of simmering longing.

"Emmy . . . Emmy . . ." He pressed frantic kisses across her eyelids and down her cheek. "I want you so desperately. I wish I could make you understand. . . ."

"I do, I do." Emmy drove her fingers through his thick hair and brought his mouth down to hers again. His tongue slipped between her lips, hot and hunting. Emmy wrapped her arms around his neck as Whit's arms came about her waist to lift her up until her feet dangled inches from the shifting sand.

As suddenly as his assault had begun, it subsided. Whit lifted his mouth from hers and set her back on her feet. He turned sharply and walked toward the surf line.

"What . . . Whit?" Emmy came up behind him and curved one hand in the crook of his arm, but he didn't turn toward her. "What's wrong?"

A mirthless laugh tumbled from him, and he shook his head and looked down at the water lapping around his tennis shoes. "I'm getting carried away. You don't live as long as I have without knowing when you're about to reach the point of no return. You told me just minutes ago that you didn't want to—"

Emmy tugged on his arm, turning him to face her. "I've changed my mind," she said, speaking for her heart and its desperation. "That's a woman's prerogative, isn't it?"

"Oh, Emmy." He smiled and pulled the hood up to cover her ebony hair. "You're such a puzzle. I'm trying to play by your rules, but you keep changing them."

"Love me, Whit." Emmy tipped up her chin, offering her lips to him and not caring that her attitude was brazen. He was right. The lid had blown off her good sense, and all she wanted was to be held and loved by him.

His kiss was light and too brief. "I'll race you to my hotel room."

Laughing, she broke away from him and sprinted in the direction of the hotel, but Whit was right behind her and overtook her with only a few long strides. He passed her, kicking up sand, and disappeared inside the hotel. Emmy charged forward, but by the time she entered the lobby Whit was nowhere in sight. She waited impatiently for the elevator, knowing that he was probably already in his room, a few doors away from her own. Her subconscious voice tried to wrestle her attention from her quest for fulfillment, but she refused to lend it an ear. She had passed the point of no return, and she knew it. For better or worse, she wanted to be with Whit tonight.

The elevator released her, and she raced down the

corridor, sidestepping dinner trays and stumbling to a halt in front of his door. She knocked, and the door opened.

"I won." Whit pulled her inside and shut the door behind her.

"What did you win?"

"You." He kissed her, his lips sliding back and forth to create a sizzling friction. Her panting made him laugh, and he stepped back. "Out of breath?"

"Yes." Emmy placed a hand over her heart, feeling its labored pounding. "Could I have a drink of water?"

"Sure." He motioned to the wet bar. "Help yourself."

While she poured herself a glass of water from the pitcher, Whit switched on the radio and found a station that played soft, romantic instrumentals. He turned to face her, and his eyes glimmered with bold intentions.

Emmy caught her breath and blindly set the glass on the table. She'd never seen a man look so attractive and so dangerous in her whole life! Every nerve in her body quivered, and her breathing became shallow as Whit closed the distance between them in three strides. He swept her up into his arms, and his mouth left a trail of fire down her throat as he carried her into the bedroom and set her down on the king-sized bed. With a springy gait that reminded her of a panther's tread, Whit went to the window and drew back the draperies to reveal the ever-changing seascape. The sight of the rolling waves sent a restless longing through Emmy, but she didn't move a muscle. She couldn't. The hunter had stalked and captured her, and the next move had to be his.

"You are the most beautiful creature I've ever seen," he whispered as his gaze roamed her face and figure. "Those eyes!" He took a ragged breath and expelled it. "How I love your eyes." He came to her, dropped to his knees and buried his face between her breasts. His arms tightened around her like steel bands, and his breath warmed her skin through the thickness of her pullover.

Emmy kissed the crown of his head, then rested her cheek against the silky texture of his hair. He smelled like an ocean breeze. His hands moved up her spine to flatten against the back of her head, and his fingers tangled in her dark hair. His mouth covered hers in a kiss that reached her soul. Emmy's tongue tasted the salt on his lips before sliding into the moist cavern of his mouth and finding the answering stroke of his tongue. Her hands moved to the side of his face and felt the hollows of his cheeks as his tongue parried with hers. She loved the feel of the light stubble against her sensitive palms.

Warmth stole under her pullover, and large hands covered her breasts. Emmy moaned and fell backward, tearing her mouth from his and arching her body upward in an instinctive plea for more contact. Whit stretched out his arms and inched up her pullover to expose the fullness of her breasts to his appreciative gaze. Emmy sensed the quickening of his excitement, which triggered a sensuous stirring within her. He thought she was beautiful and desirable; his expression told her so. His fingertips tapped across her puckering nipples, spreading fire into her veins. He pushed himself up until his mouth could take one of the tight buds inside, and his tongue rolled across it. Emmy gasped at the flames of desire that coursed through her, and shut her eyes tightly as Whit's tongue continued its exquisite torture. He moved his attention to the other breast, then kissed each straining nipple in turn before he flicked them with the tip of his tongue. Emmy writhed and sucked in her breath.

She sat up and helped him remove her pullover, shorts and tennis shoes. Whit stripped off his shirt and soggy shoes, then stretched out on his side and brought her lips to his again for a series of light, nibbling kisses that left her breathless and ready for more.

"Whit . . . Whit," Emmy whispered between sipping kisses, "I want you. Oh, how I want you." Her fingers brushed across his jeans, then settled unerringly on the evidence of his arousal. Whit's body tensed, and Emmy wasn't sure whether he was even breathing. She opened her eyes and saw the fire in his. "Let me see you. Let me touch you." She tugged at the snap and zipper before Whit shoved aside her hand, stood up and shed the rest of his clothes.

His body was glorious. Spellbinding. Emmy propped herself up on her elbows and memorized every inch of it from the wedge of his shoulders to his hair-roughened legs. Her gaze moved up slowly, stopping here and—oh, yes!—*there* before taking in the width of his chest, liberally covered with fine, dark hair, and then his square jaw and burning gaze. She reached out and touched him, and he seemed to grow in her hand.

Whit settled a knee on the bed, then covered her body with his. His weight pressed her into the mattress, making her feel as if she were wrapped tightly in a cocoon of flesh and fabric. His lips and tongue danced across her breasts as one hand moved between her thighs. His fingers worked magic, rubbing and massaging and invading her. She arched closer, trembling and aching for the true joining of their passion.

Suddenly his roving fingers were replaced by a spear of molten fire. Emmy clutched at his shoulders as her eyes opened wide, only to close again in sweet relief. It was everything she had expected and more. Whit's passion was a raging tempest that swept through her like a hurricane. The push and pull of him was pure ecstasy, and she could do nothing but hold on and utter sounds of wonder and awe at the feelings and white-hot emotions he created within her.

Whit straightened his arms, letting them take his weight, and stared down into Emmy's face, which reflected exactly what he was feeling. She clutched at him, enveloping him in her warmly passionate embrace. Tension grew within him until he felt like a taut violin string. He threw back his head and shut his eyes, trying to hold on to the feeling for a few more precious seconds. Emmy trembled, sending spasms through him, and her sounds of pleasure rolled over him and brought a smile to his lips. He had waited years to hear those sounds from her . . . years to please her . . . years to be pleased by her. Surely not even a chorus of angels could sound as sweet.

"Oh, Whit . . . I . . . Whit!"

He opened his eyes and saw that she was whipping her head from side to side in silent adulation. Tears glistened in the corners of her eyes, and he lowered himself to lick them away, then kiss her eyelids.

"Are you okay?" he asked, suddenly concerned when she released a little sob.

"Yes, yes." Her voice was a raspy whisper. "Now, Whit. Now."

Her hips moved ever so slightly, but it was enough to send him over the brink. He tumbled into the black abyss of fulfillment, and his body jerked into hers again and again. He heard himself making hoarse, strange sounds as he spun out of control and fell into the lap of repletion. Gradually he became aware of the sheen of perspiration that covered his body, the rasping sound of his breathing and the diminishing demands of his passion.

Emmy laced her hands behind his neck and pulled him down so that she could press kisses across his forehead, his eyelids, his moist lips. She was stunned by the beauty of it all. Good heavens, what had she and Jerry been doing all those nights? Whatever it was, it couldn't compare to this. Whit had changed her whole concept of lovemaking. He was still inside her, motionless now and tame, but she was careful not to lose him. She hugged him closer, letting her hands roam across his shoulder blades, the curve of his spine and the tight bunching of muscles in his hips.

"I don't want to move . . . ever."

Whit laughed softly and opened his eyes. "Ever?"

"At least not for days."

The curve of her neck tempted him, and he kissed the creamy skin and spoke against it. "Give me a few minutes and let's see what happens."

"Take your time," Emmy murmured. "I'm not going anywhere."

Emmy pulled Whit's robe closer to her body and leaned her forehead against the cool glass. The sun climbed higher into the sky, and she guessed that it must be close to ten o'clock. She sensed Whit's approach, but didn't turn to face him. His arms came around her waist, and he pulled her back against him.

"What time is that interview today?"

"Two. We have plenty of time. Are you hungry? I can order up breakfast."

"Later." Emmy edged away when his lips moved against the side of her neck.

"Emmy?" He stepped to one side and pulled her around to face him. "Uh-oh. Are you having morning misgivings?"

She smiled at his description. "In a way, I suppose."

"Don't." He kissed the tip of her nose. "Please, don't."

Emmy took a deep breath. Whit was fresh from the shower, and he smelled of lime soap. "Whit, I've been trying to think of a way to explain to you how I feel . . . but I . . ." She shook her head.

"I'll wait. You don't have to explain anything to me, you know."

She shrugged and moved away from him to stare out the window again. "My vocabulary is woefully inadequate."

"Show me. Who needs words at a time like this?"

She rewarded him with a tiny smile. "I do." She watched the waves again, and the growing number of sunbathers. "Last night changed my whole concept of . . . of what a man can mean to a woman. I thought I knew myself, but now I'm not so sure."

"Let's go back to bed."

"No." She shook her head firmly.

Whit sat on the arm of a chair, a confused expression on his face. "Okay, Emmy. I'm trying to understand what you're telling me, but I'm afraid—"

"So am I." Blue eyes collided with brown ones. "That's it, Whit. I'm afraid."

"Of what? Me? You?"

"Partly me, but mainly us." She crossed her arms, feeling Whit's intent stare and his confusion. "I wasn't myself last night. I don't know who I was, just that it wasn't me . . . or at least I didn't recognize myself." The words to explain began forming in her mind, but she didn't know if they'd make any sense to Whit. Somehow, she needed to voice them, regardless. "I've never made love to anyone other than Jerry, and I didn't make love with him until after we were married. Since my divorce I haven't wanted to sleep with anyone. It just never crossed my mind until last night . . . with you." She gathered a breath and let it go in a long sigh. "But I don't know why I wanted you. I don't know if I love you, or if I just wanted to be loved."

"Emmy, you're blowing this out of proportion."

"Maybe it seems that way to you. Everything has happened so fast that I don't know where I'm coming from or where I'm going. Until I know why I slept with you last night, I can't sleep with you again."

"Emmy, for pity's sake!"

She looked at his scowling face, then quickly away. "I have to know why I threw aside my inhibitions and my principles last night. I have to know if I came to you out of pure lust, or out of love. I know it's not important to you, but it is to me."

"It is important to me."

Emmy sought out his gaze and discovered that he was stating a simple truth. "It is?"

"Yes, it is." He stood up and walked over to the bed, gazing down at the crumpled sheets.

"What I'd like to do right now is get dressed and go to my room. I need to get myself together before the interview," she said softly.

He nodded. "I understand."

Emmy's heart swelled with an unknown emotion. "Whittier Hayes, you are the most understanding man I've ever met."

He smiled and chuckled under his breath. "To be honest, Emmy, most of the time when I say I understand, I haven't the slightest idea what you're talking about. However, in this case, I think you should have some time to yourself before the interview." He massaged the back of his neck with one hand. "I'd like some time alone, too."

"Thanks."

His gaze explored her face for a few moments before he nodded toward the bathroom. "Go ahead and get dressed. I'll be in the other room." He went toward the sitting room, but stopped and turned back to her. His expression was fathomless, but there was a hint of sadness in his eyes. He started to say something, thought better of it and closed the door behind him, leaving her alone with her own thoughts.

Whit sat on the divan and stared at the roiling ocean. She didn't know whether or not she loved him. How long would it take for her to be sure of her feelings, and what if she decided she didn't love him? What then? Would he be able to live with that? Could he stand by and watch his dreams die?

He blinked his eyes and his lashes grew wet as he continued his moody examination of the North Atlantic.

7

Dear T.C.,

You have a right to be confused. Susie threw those flowers in your face? Are you telling me everything?

You've liked Susie for a long time, so don't give up after only a few weeks. Be her friend by giving her the benefit of the doubt. Tell her you'd like to help her over the rough spots in her life and be the man she can lean on.

No woman in her right mind would throw flowers in the face of such an honest, loving, kind gentleman. I can't imagine what has gotten into Susie. Maybe she just had a bad day. Give her another chance, T.C., and let her know that you're going to be around for the duration.

Maudie

Emmy folded the New Orleans newspaper and placed it on the bureau. Good old reliable Bertha. She'd followed the instructions and made sure that the letter and its answer were printed as soon as possible. She hoped this bit of advice would do the trick for poor Torch Carrier.

She looked around the room, thinking that it wasn't that much different from the one in Miami except that this one's color scheme was bright—pastels instead of Miami's earth tones.

Fresh from the shower, dressed only in her bra, panties and a half slip, Emmy sat at the dresser and gazed questioningly at her reflection in the oval mirror.

Who was that woman? she wondered. What did she want? What did she need? She'd like a nickel for every time she had heard *"You're* Maudie? But you're nothing like I expected!" Recently, that exclamation—or something close to it—had replaced the customary "Nice to meet you." What *had* they expected? A tottering grandmother-type who clucked her tongue at all the headstrong young folks? A nosey, middle-aged aunt-type who loved to dish dirt with the rest of the "girls"?

Emmy smiled wistfully at her mirror twin. Funny how certain names conjured up certain types. Maybe that's why she had grabbed her nickname and held on for dear life.

Emmy picked up a brush and began arranging her hair in a Victorian-era bundle on the crown of her head, freeing a few tendrils at her ears and nape. She took longer than usual in applying her makeup, all the while keeping an eye on the time. Whit had invited her to go "out on the town" this evening, and she had been looking forward to it all day. Since their night in Miami, Whit had retreated from her. During her two days in Atlanta, Emmy hadn't heard from until he'd called to confirm their flight to New Orleans, but she had enjoyed the respite. After Miami she had been in turmoil, and it was all she could do to keep her mind on her work.

However, during the respite from Whit, she had found no answers. Did she love him, or did she just desire him? She had certainly enjoyed her night of lovemaking with him. It had been a revelation, a miracle, a milestone in her life. She knew she had loved Jerry, but now she knew that she had never wanted him with the intensity she had wanted Whittier Hayes. It was as if she had been holding back—keeping most of herself in reserve—for one special night when she could give her all. Remembering the afterglow of that experience, Emmy shivered. She had wished she could stay in his arms forever in peaceful oblivion, because she had known even then that the next hours would bring questions, doubts and confusion.

With Jerry she had always been satiated, but with Whit she had wanted more and more.

In college she had always been aware of Whit Hayes— and wary. Had she known even then that he was a dangerous predator? Had she sensed that he was the man who could unleash a wild, wanting part of her? It was frightening to discover such traits in herself at this stage in life.

"Am I in love with him?" she asked her mirror image. "What does he feel for me? Am I a captive or a victor?"

Emmy stood up and went to the bed, where she had draped the dress she would wear this evening. She smoothed her fingers along the beige Irish handkerchief linen, and examined the draped neckline, long sleeves and revealing draped back. It had cost too much, but she had loved the way she felt in it, so she had bought it with little more than a wince when she'd written the check. Emmy slipped into the dress, zipped it up and turned to look at the scooped oval that revealed her creamy back to the waist. She clipped cultured pearls to her earlobes, and fastened a string of pearls and diamonds around her neck.

"Perfect," Emmy declared, then jumped slightly at the sound of someone tapping lightly at her door.

She sprayed a floral perfume lavishly at her wrists and throat before hurrying to answer the summons. Her foolish heart stilled, then climbed into her throat at the sight of Whit. His light gray linen suit was double-breasted and harked back to the Roaring Twenties. His white shirt drew attention to the white carnation in his lapel, and his thin dark gray tie was secured by a silvery mother-of-pearl tie bar.

"I've missed you," she said breathlessly, then wished she had thought before she'd spoken when Whit gave a startled lift of his brows.

"Missed me? I just saw you"—he flicked back a cuff to check his watch—"three hours ago."

She laughed, wanting to kick herself, and grabbed her evening purse from the table. "I'm ready."

"And willing?"

Emmy's gaze met his, and she knew that her surprise registered on her face. It was the first suggestive thing he'd said to her since Miami, and relief poured through her. Was he going to be more than just her old friend tonight? Was that mischievous, cunning hunter back on the trail?

He saved her from answering by gently seizing her elbow and guiding her from the room into the corridor. "Got your key?"

"Yes."

Whit closed the door and fell into step with her. "You look lovely this evening. New dress?"

"I bought it a year ago, but I've only worn it once before tonight. You look dapper. Your suit reminds me of something from an old movie about gangsters and con artists."

"Gangsters and con artists." He stroked his smooth jaw and squinted one eye in thoughtful contemplation. "I'm not quite sure if that's a compliment."

"It was meant to be." On impulse, Emmy straightened the carnation in his lapel.

"You aren't allergic to it, are you?"

"No." She smiled and sniffed the lacy-edged flower. "In fact, carnations are my favorite. Where are we going for dinner?"

"I've made reservations at Delmonico's." He stepped into the elevator with her, but didn't press the lobby button immediately. Instead he touched her arm and drew her gaze to his. "This will be an evening to remember for both of us. New Orleans is a special city. Are you ready and willing for an evening of fabulous food, colorful sights, friendly people and a dash of *lagniappe?*"

"What's that?" she asked, not trusting herself enough to pronounce the strange word.

Whit leaned forward until his lips brushed her temple. *"Lagniappe,"* he repeated. "That elusive something . . . that added, unprescribed measure that pops up where and when you least expect it." His lips pressed a tender kiss to her forehead, then skimmed down the side of her face to the pearl at her earlobe. She felt him kiss the white orb before the tip of his tongue moistened the skin behind her ear. Emmy shivered and gasped, her head jerking backward and her eyes growing wider in surprise. Whit laughed softly and reached out to push the correct button on the panel without even looking at it. His eyes glittered with dark secrets as he whispered, "*Lagniappe,* Emmy. It's the stuff of life."

Emmy faced front, suddenly quiveringly aware of him and the spell he was casting. For her the evening was already memorable, and she hadn't even left the hotel yet.

Whit plucked the carnation from his lapel and tossed it into the sparkling waters of the fountain across the street from Jackson Square. The white flower bobbed on the surface, pushed this way and that by the cascading water. He looked up and stared moodily at the majesty of the square.

Emmy followed his gaze and feasted on one of America's most famous attractions. Andrew Jackson, astride a rearing horse, tipped his bronze hat in homage to the heart of the French Quarter. St. Louis Cathedral's three steeples seemed to hold up the star-studded sky and keep it from draping around the neighboring Cabildo and Presbytère. The night was fragrant with the scent of spring, its green beauty veiled by the evening's dark light.

Behind them the Mississippi River cut through the land, giving birth to a number of huge cities that had prospered, fallen and risen again. But it was Jackson Square that drew the eye and tickled the imagination. Historic buildings sprang from the rich earth in mute testimony to fantasies, fortunes and failures.

New Orleans's history had made peace with the

present in an inspiring combination that attracted tourists by the droves, and Emmy was glad to count herself as one of them. She examined the area that had once been a dusty parade ground, appreciating all that had happened here. Jackson Square was the heart of it all; the very center of the Vieux Carré.

"If that square could talk, the stories it could tell," Whit whispered in obvious reverence. "It gives me chills to think of the people who have walked across those grounds. Jean and Pierre Lafitte, Carry Nation, Marie Laveau, William—"

"Marie Laveau?" Emmy asked, seizing on the exotic name.

"Yes, she was the most powerful voodoo queen. Some say her spirit lives in the square to give peace to the downtrodden."

"Why do I get the feeling this is one of your favorite cities?"

Whit smiled. "Aside from Atlanta, it is. Both cities are drenched in history, but here it's more apparent. In many ways it looks the same as it did back in the early 1800s. The burning of Atlanta destroyed so much of our legacy. It's a pity."

"Are you a history buff?"

He slanted her a curious glance. "Being Southern goes hand in hand with loving history, doesn't it?"

"Yes, I suppose so. I grew up hearing about the Civil War as if it had occurred only a few years ago."

Whit stuck his hands into his trouser pockets and looked toward the bustling Café du Monde. "Let's top off the evening with some *café au lait* and *beignets.*" He cocked his elbow, and Emmy curved her hand in the crook of his arm.

"I'm still stuffed from dinner. That shrimp creole was delicious."

"You should have tasted my shrimp remoulade." Whit smacked his lips and sighed. "If I lived here I'd be the size of a blimp. It's a good thing I only visit a few times a year."

"My weakness isn't the food," Emmy admitted. "It's the music. I adore jazz. Thanks for indulging me tonight. How many clubs did we hit? At least six."

"Eight." Whit shrugged and guided her to an empty table that provided a view of Jackson Square. "But who's counting?" He sat down across from her and glanced toward the street. Something caught his attention, and he frowned. "Look at that car."

Emmy searched the street and saw the object of his attention. The white car was speckled with squashed insects. "What happened to it?"

"Lovebugs."

"Oh, I've heard of those. There are swarms of them this time of year."

"Yes, and if you leave them on your car they can corrode the finish. A nasty souvenir of New Orleans."

"Why do they call them lovebugs?"

Whit grinned. "Because they're swarming to make love, and they do it in midair. They're amazing little termites."

The waiter approached the table, and Whit ordered their coffee and *beignets*.

"I've heard of this place, too," Emmy said, glancing around the famous coffee shop. It was open-air, with a definite Old World charm that was increased by the horses and buggies that lined the streets in search of tourists. "Can we take a buggy ride back to the hotel?"

"Sure, if you want."

"I want."

The waiter returned with their midnight treat. Aromatic steam curled up from the coffee, chicory and hot milk mixture, and the square French doughnuts tempted Emmy's sweet tooth. She reached for one, but Whit stopped her.

"Let me show you the correct way to consume these." He tucked a paper napkin under his collar and positioned it carefully over his shirtfront and tie, then selected one of the doughnuts, holding it between his thumb and forefinger. He bit into it, then brushed powdered sugar off the napkin. "You see? It's bite and brush, bite and brush."

Emmy laughed. "I've got the hang of it." She imitated him, making him laugh. "Mmmm. These are delicious! I could eat a dozen."

"I thought that jazz was your weakness?"

"That was before I tasted one of these." She took a sip of the coffee, and her eyes widened. "And the coffee!" She looked around and spotted the display she'd seen on the way inside. "I'm going to buy a pound of this and make it at home."

"It won't taste the same," Whit warned. "I've tried to reproduce it, but I've come to the conclusion that you have to be sitting here to enjoy it."

"Could it be la—la—"

"Lagniappe," Whit said, then repeated it slowly so that she could catch the sound of it. *"Lan-yap."*

"Lan-yap."

"Right, and it certainly could be what's missing when you're back in Atlanta and trying to capture the flavor of New Orleans."

"Excuse me."

Emmy looked up to find that a woman was hovering

near her. The woman was dressed in a bright red dress that matched her hair, and her green eyes were wide with hope.

"Aren't you Maudie? The one who writes the lovelorn column?"

"Yes, I am." Emmy glanced at Whit and saw that he was enjoying the interruption.

"I thought so! I saw your picture in the paper today. I'm Naughty in New Orleans."

"Naughty in—?" Emmy snapped her fingers. "Your the lady who—"

"Was attracted to my daughter's intended," the woman finished, then held out her hand. "Prudence Boop. Pru to my friends."

Emmy shook her hand. "Nice to meet you. Did my advice work?"

"And how!" Pru rolled her green eyes. "My daughter isn't speaking to me. She moved to San Francisco to get away from me!"

"Oh." Emmy looked at Whit and saw that he was avidly following the conversation. She faced the woman again, trying to remember her exact advice. Surely, she hadn't told this woman to sever her relationship with her daughter! "So you took up with your daughter's boyfriend?"

"Yes." Pru heaved a sigh and looked across the restaurant at a young man who was sitting alone and giving her the eye. He was attractive, but looked world-weary. "What a mistake. I thought he'd be a firecracker in bed, but was I wrong! I feel like a sex surrogate. The kid doesn't know anything!"

Whit chuckled and covered his smile with one hand.

"Well, I don't want to make a nuisance of myself. I just wanted to meet you face-to-face. I never dreamed you'd be so pretty!" Pru glanced at Whit, then back to Emmy. "I'll leave you and your husband or lover or—"

"He's not my—" Emmy began.

"Then he should be," Pru interrupted with a lift of her flame-colored brows. "Good night, y'all." She whirled in a swish of red chiffon and rejoined the sad-eyed young man.

"Can you beat that?" Whit asked with a chuckle. "What a character."

"She missed the point I was trying to make," Emmy explained. "Maudie told her to think through her situation carefully and decide which person meant more to her—her daughter or her daughter's boyfriend. I never expected her to choose the man over her own flesh and blood!"

"Some people are pretty thick-headed when it comes to sex," Whit said with a slight frown.

An uneasiness stole through Emmy, and she looked away from the woman and her young escort. "She's the kind of woman I never want to become. I don't want to be with a man just because he's a . . . a . . ."

"Firecracker in bed?" Whit supplied.

"Yes." Emmy stared blindly into her coffee cup and jumped slightly when Whit's hand covered hers on the table.

"You could never be that type of woman, Emmy." He squeezed her hand, then let go. "By the way, I refused an interview on a talk show here on your behalf."

"Why? I thought that was the purpose of this trip."

"It is, but only when it's beneficial. The host of the show would make fun of your book instead of encouraging people to buy it. It's better if we steer clear of him."

Emmy set her cup down with a thump. "I could have handled him."

"No, I think I made the right decision. He would have made you look like a fool."

"And just how could he have done that?" Emmy challenged, not liking the certainty in Whit's tone.

"Simply by reading some of the more outrageous letters aloud and then reading your advice and making fun of it. I've seen him in action, Emmy. He's into ridicule, and you'd be asking for trouble if you agreed to be a guest on his show."

Emmy squared her shoulders and adopted a confident posture. "I'll have you know that my advice is good and sound." She glared at Whit when he shot her a dubious glance. "Isn't it? Whit! Isn't my advice right on the money?"

Whit laughed softly under his breath and averted his gaze, preferring to stare at the fidgeting horses along the curb. "Sometimes your advice is right on the money," he answered slowly, "and sometimes it isn't worth two cents."

Emmy stiffened and felt her temper flare. "You might handle my publicity, Whittier Hayes, but you don't handle my business or the way I conduct it. I've done quite well without your pointed observations, thank you very much!"

She thought he would have an angry retaliation, but he surprised her by grinning in delight. He fished a few bills from his pocket and tossed them onto the table.

"Come on. Let's hire a buggy to take us back to the hotel."

They left the Café du Monde, and Whit handed Emmy into one of the carriages. The driver clucked his tongue, setting the black horse in motion, and the steed's hooves clicked against the street on the way to the Royal Sonesta Hotel on Bourbon Street.

Emmy tried to enjoy the experience, but Whit's evaluation of her advice still rankled her. She glanced at him from time to time, but he seemed immersed in the passing scenery. Having decided that this trip would be made in silence, Emmy jerked slightly when Whit broke through the quiet tension.

"Emmy?"

"Yes?" She was immediately alert, having noted the wondering quality in his voice. What now? Did he have another pearl of wisdom for her?

"Haven't you ever wished for someone who would take care of you and give *you* advice for a change? You know . . . a strong shoulder to lean on, so to speak."

"Certainly not!" She crossed her arms and glared at the passing cars. Why in the world would he think she wanted that? "The last person who tried to manage my life almost ruined it. I can take care of myself."

"Jerry?"

"Jerry." Emmy frowned, then swept aside the memories. "I'm not a weakling. I don't need anyone's shoulder but my own."

Whit shook his head and laughed, finally drawing Emmy's smoldering gaze to his. She gave him a murderous glare.

"What's so funny?" she demanded between clenched teeth.

"You," he managed between chuckles. "At times, dear Emmy, you're a riot."

"I'm glad you find me so amusing," she said with brittle sarcasm.

The carriage bumped to a halt in front of the hotel, and Emmy scrambled down to the sidewalk, not waiting for Whit's assistance. He caught up with her at the entrance, but stood back a little and grinned.

"Aren't you going to open the door for me?" he taunted. "Don't you want to exercise your superiority—your independence?"

Emmy was sure that smoke must be escaping through her ears as she whipped open the door and let him precede her into the lobby. They took the elevator up to the fourth floor, and Emmy hurried toward her room, which was next to Whit's. She unlocked the door, went inside and turned to find that Whit had followed her into the sitting room.

"It's been a nice evening, Whit, but I'm tired and—" Her excuses were cut off by the grinding pressure of his mouth on hers.

Emmy managed a sound of surprise before his arms circled her waist and hauled her roughly against him. She tore her mouth from his and pushed her fists into his chest.

"Whit, what do you think you're doing?"

"Staying," he said, succinctly and seductively. "That's what I'm doing. You want me here."

"No, I don't."

His lips flamed across hers again, and his tongue was rough velvet in her mouth.

"You want me here," he repeated.

"No, I—" Moist lips killed the rest of her words and moved gently back and forth until she opened her mouth to his agile tongue.

"You want me."

"No." Emmy moaned softly as his mouth took hers again, and she felt her resistance melt under the searing onslaught.

"You—want—me," he repeated slowly.

"Yes!" Emmy pulled his head down, and her lips parted in submission. Whit's arms tightened at her waist, and he lifted her up until she was standing on air. She felt as if she were floating as he walked toward the bedroom. He set her on her feet, and his hands found the fastener at her back.

The sensuous scrape of the zipper sent a thrill of anticipation through Emmy. She pushed the jacket off his shoulders and down his arms, then loosened the knot of his tie. Her hands trembled as she continued to undress him, and passion built by inches until she was shaking with impatience. Whit removed her dress and tossed it into a chair, then stepped back to let her finish the task while he stripped off the rest of his clothes. He was faster than she was, and he pushed her back onto the bed before she could remove her lace-and-satin panties.

He kissed her hard on the mouth as his fingers inched under the elastic band. His lips traveled down her body to where his hands were slowly revealing her most intimate part. He tossed aside the strip of lacy satin, and his mouth settled between her thighs. His tongue touched her, and Emmy's hips jerked involuntarily.

"Yes, oh, yes!" Emmy combed her fingers through his hair and pressed his mouth closer to the flash point of her desire. He kissed her there, and the kiss reverberated throughout her body. She slipped under his spell and flowered beneath his raining kisses and stroking hands.

Desire raged through her, tearing apart her earlier misgivings and releasing that wild part of her that she had tried to tame. The room spun before her glazed eyes as she sat astride him and experienced feelings she had never known before. His fingers moved from her waist to her hair and sought out the remaining pins until it fell heavily to her shoulders.

"Oh, Emmy . . ." His voice floated to her, hoarse and strained. "That's it . . . that's it." His hands found her waist again to guide her into a grinding dance of passion that made him cry out her name in a beseeching way.

The world exploded around her in embers of brightness. Whit shuddered into her, and Emmy balanced herself precariously while her body convulsed with everlasting desire. When she opened her eyes it was to study the face of the man she loved. Why had she ever doubted that? she wondered. Loving him was something she was certain of now, something so natural that she wondered if there had been a time when she had not loved him. Even back in college . . . even then?

Emmy bent over and kissed his mouth tenderly. He opened his eyes, letting her see the beauty of his soul and how deeply she had touched him. She pressed soft, clinging kisses to his lips while her fingertips explored his high cheekbones, feathery lashes, and perfectly shaped ears. Peace filled her, a sweet peace that she hadn't felt in a long, long time. She was no longer afraid of the part of her that was wild and wanton, because she knew that love had unleashed it. Love, not lust. Oh, how she loved this man!

She stretched out on her side and leaned her cheek into his shoulder. Her hand moved through the silky hair on his chest and traced its intricate pattern. His eyes were closed, and his breathing was still rapid. As she watched, a grin lifted one side of his mouth, and he opened his eyes and stared at the shadowed ceiling.

"That was . . ."

"*Lagniappe,*" she whispered, and Whit laughed.

8

Dear Maudie,

I have come to the conclusion that Susie doesn't know what she wants. She says she wants one thing, but she really wants something entirely different. If I sound confused it's because I am!

I've followed your advice to the letter, but my relationship with Susie has become more muddled. In the past, I've always acted on instinct around women. Should I rely on my instincts in this case? Susie is too important to lose. If I can't have her as a lover, I want to keep her as a friend.

I've made a little progress since my last letter, but not enough to ensure Susie's love. What do you think? Should I play it by ear and see what happens?

Torch Carrier

Emmy hung up the telephone and sighed. Bertha was really hung up on Torch Carrier's problems, she thought. Every time she got a letter from him, she couldn't wait to phone Emmy and read it, then demand a reply as soon as possible because "we can't keep him hanging in midair!"

But Emmy had other problems on her mind today. She wandered over to the table that held the remains of her breakfast and poured herself another cup of coffee. Picking up the note Whit had left her, she read it again and frowned at the overall tone of it. Bossy, she thought. He's a very bossy man.

" 'Dearest Emmy,' " she read aloud. " 'Last night was a dream come true. I didn't want to wake you, so I slipped out to keep an early appointment with a few area newspaper reporters. Instructions for this morning are to rest, have a hearty breakfast and think of me. Follow them implicitly. See you around noon. Yours, Whit.' "

Emmy folded the letter and tucked it into her purse. She tried to think of Whit's good qualities—which were abundant—instead of his bad qualities—which were few, but troublesome.

Finishing her second cup of coffee, Emmy sat down at the table and patted her stomach. She had taken his advice—well, *advice* was too tame a word—his *order* to have a hearty breakfast, but she didn't want to rest. She felt younger this morning. Younger and more beautiful. Emmy stretched her arms above her head as a lazy, self-indulgent smile spread across her lips. Last night *had* been a dream come true. Whit was a consummate lover and, she admitted to herself with a little laugh, she wasn't chopped liver. Together they were magic, communicating

135

with each other in a silent, ancient language known only by the most perfectly matched lovers. A woman didn't need a wealth of experience to know instinctively when she had met her match, her emotional equal. With Jerry, Emmy had experienced the lows which made her more attuned to the highs she had found with Whit.

Thinking of all the lonely and troubled people she had corresponded with over the years, Emmy felt a sadness for them that she hadn't felt before, followed by a realization of how truly lucky she was to have found Whittier Hayes again. What an incredible stroke of luck for him to have walked back into her life! Oh, she was blessed.

She had discovered a different side of Whit last night, a more aggressive, take-charge side that she had thoroughly enjoyed. He had orchestrated the evening from the moment he had appeared at her door to the last kiss he had pressed to her lips before she had tumbled into a dreamless slumber. And what a maestro! The night had been a symphony of passion, and Whit had conducted it masterfully. He had said it would be a night to remember, and Emmy knew that she would never forget one second of it. When she thought of New Orleans she would always think of Whit . . . that night . . . their love.

Emmy released a tiny sigh. Yes, she liked his aggression in bed, but not out of it. One way to get the message across to him was for her to show aggression. She smiled thoughtfully when she recalled a snatch of advice her mother had given her when Emmy had returned from her honeymoon with Jerry.

"Listen to me, Maude Edith," her mother had warned. "Don't start off this marriage by spoiling Jerry rotten. New brides usually make that tragic mistake. When the blush is off the rose, he'll still expect to be pampered, and you'll have only yourself to blame for that. For heaven's sake, start on an equal footing with him."

Too bad she hadn't heeded her mother's advice, Emmy thought. She had spoiled Jerry, and he had taken advantage of it. This time she *would* start on an equal footing. Whit had to learn that she loved him, wanted him, but that she didn't *need* him in every aspect of her life. Maybe she should talk to him about her problems with Jerry. Maybe that would make him understand why it was so important that she hold on to her independence where her business was concerned. Surely he'd understand that she didn't want another bossy husband.

Husband? Emmy sat straighter and felt her eyes widen. Whoa, girl! she cautioned herself. Don't go putting the cart before the horse. After all, Whit had never said he loved her. He'd implied it, but an implication was worth two cents these days.

Two cents. Emmy stood up, feeling the shadow of her earlier anger when Whit had said that her advice was worth that measly amount. He'd told her that he was a fan of her column. How could he be a fan and have such a dismal evaluation of her talent?

The ringing telephone shattered her contemplative mood, and she hurried to answer it, thinking that it was probably Bertha or Whit.

"Hello?"

"Ms. Bakersfield, please."

"Speaking."

"Please hold for Mr. Dan Carter."

"Okay." Emmy sat on the bed and wondered who Dan Carter could be. A fan? Someone she had met at the autograph party?

"Ms. Bakersfield?" The voice was brisk and self-confident.

"Yes, this is she."

"Dan Carter here. I'm the host of 'Carter's Corner.'"

"'Carter's Corner'?"

"Yes, the local program you were unable to be a guest on."

"Oh, yes." Emmy nodded absently. Must be the fellow Whit had warned her about.

"I've had a last-minute cancellation for today's show, and I'm calling to ask you one more time if you'd agree to do a guest spot. My show has high ratings and could sell a lot of books for you."

"Well, I . . ."

"Your front man told me that your schedule was full, so I'll understand if you can't squeeze it in. There's another author in town, a gal who wrote an exercise book, so—"

"I can do it." Emmy jumped slightly, surprised by her snap decision.

"Fine." Dan Carter almost purred the word, like a cat who had swallowed a canary. "We'll need you at the studio by eleven-thirty, so that doesn't give you much time. It's ten-thirty now."

"I'll be there, and thanks for asking me again. I appreciate it."

Carter chuckled and, for some reason, the sound made the hairs on the back of Emmy's neck stand on end. "Sure thing, Ms. Bakersfield. I'm looking forward to . . . talking to you. I'll send a limo for you. Say in about forty minutes?"

"Yes, I'll be ready."

Dan Carter hung up, and Emmy frowned, thinking that the man was just short of being rude. But she had no time to analyze him. She had to get a move on if she wanted to get to the studio in time. She had forty minutes to make herself presentable, leave Whit a note and—

Emmy's thoughts skidded to a halt. Whit! The fine hairs at the nape of her neck lifted again. Would he be angry? Maybe she shouldn't have accepted the interview. Maybe she should call Dan Carter back and—

No. Emmy strode toward the bathroom and turned on the shower. This would be a sign to Whit that she had a mind of her own and that she used it!

Whit glanced at the note again and crumpled it in his hand. Damn her for going against his advice! He glared past the cab driver's shoulder at the congested traffic. He'd never make it to the studio in time to stop her. She was a lamb going to the slaughter, and she didn't even know it! Carter would make mincemeat out of her.

"How much farther?" Whit asked, leaning forward, as if his shifted weight would make the taxi go faster.

"It's about a half a block up there." The cabbie pointed straight ahead, then applied the brakes when a traffic light switched to red.

"Here." Whit shoved a five dollar bill over the man's shoulder. "I'll walk the rest of the way."

"Okay." The driver took the bill and glanced at it.

"Keep the change."

"Thanks, mister."

Whit slammed the door behind him and sprinted along the sidewalk, sliding to a stop before a revolving door. He glanced up at the station's call letters before pushing through the door and into the lobby. A pretty receptionist with platinum blond hair looked up in surprise.

"What studio is Carter using?" Whit demanded.

"Studio 4-A on three," the woman said, then reached out a hand when he started toward the stairs. "But you can't go in there! The show has already started!"

Whit grimaced and bounded up the stairs. He was too

late. All he could do now was stand back and watch the massacre. A couple of men stood outside the studio, and one placed a detaining hand on Whit's sleeve.

"We're on the air, sir," he said, tightening his grip.

"I'm Emmy Bakersfield's publicity agent. I'm supposed to be in there."

"Oh? Got some identification?"

Whit sighed and withdrew his wallet, flipping it open to his business card. "Satisfied?"

"Sure." The man let go of him. "Go on in, but be quiet."

Whit pushed through the double doors and blinked at the contrast between the darkness he stepped into and the pool of light in the center of the large room. Dan Carter sat in an orange chair, a benevolent smile gracing his face as he looked at Emmy, who sat opposite him. Whit smothered a groan as he tiptoed forward to stand a few feet behind one of the cameramen. Emmy looked cool and confident in a lavender blouse and matching skirt. She returned Carter's smile and laughed at something he had said.

Carter looked to be in his forties, a slick customer with carefully coiffed black hair, a thin black mustache and shifty blue eyes. He was dressed in a dark suit, white shirt and red tie. He held a few sheets of paper in his hands, and the overhead lights reflected off a big diamond on his right ring finger.

"Do you take your own advice?" Carter asked in a voice that was as oily as his hair.

"I try to," Emmy answered, her smile deepening. "I think that if you dish it out, you ought to be able to take it."

Carter glanced at the notes in his lap. "Don't you think that most of the people who write you are a little nuts?"

"No." Emmy's smile waned. "I feel compassion for them. Everyone has problems, but—"

"Everyone doesn't expect an instant cure from a complete stranger," Carter cut in. "You said you try to take your own advice."

"That's right."

"But you're divorced. Your own marriage failed, so isn't this a case of the blind leading the blind?"

Whit put a hand in front of his face, covering his eyes for a moment so that he wouldn't have to see Emmy's stiffened posture and slight wince. Here it comes. Get ready, Emmy. You asked for this, damn it. He removed his hand and saw the remnants of shock on her face. Her lips moved several times before she summoned her husky voice.

"I learned valuable lessons from my marriage and divorce, lessons I can pass on to others. I wouldn't be as effective if I lived the life of a hermit and didn't experience all the highs and lows everyone else does." She stared straight at Carter, and her eyes narrowed a fraction. "Have you ever been married?"

"We're not here to discuss me, Ms. Bakers—"

"But I'm interested," Emmy cut in, leaning toward him as if anxious for the kill. "Are you married?"

"I'm divorced." Carter ran a finger along his collar and tugged.

"You're divorced," Emmy repeated.

"That's right." Carter sat straighter and cleared his throat. "But I'm not dishing out advice to—"

"Your first divorce, is it?"

One corner of Whit's mouth edged up. Was she baiting him? Carter was obviously feeling the heat. Even from Whit's vantage point, he could see beads of perspiration on the man's upper lip.

"No, not my first." Carter swallowed hard. "My third."

The cameraman in front of Whit glanced at the other cameraman and rolled his eyes.

"Your third." Emmy repeated for effect. "Mr. Carter, you haven't learned your lessons very well. You're supposed to learn from your mistakes. I guess that's why I'm giving advice and you're not."

The cameraman chuckled and gave a thumbs up sign to the other camera operator. Whit hid his own smile behind his hand. Way to go, Emmy, he cheered silently. Now don't let him off the hook. Don't give him an inch.

Carter shuffled through the notes on his lap, frowning his displeasure at Emmy's pointed observation. "One of the novel things about your column is that you follow up on your advice by encouraging your pen pals to write back and let you know how or if they solved their problems."

"That's correct." Emmy sat back and crossed her shapely legs. She smiled confidently. "People usually write me back. If my advice doesn't work, then I suggest other tactics."

"Like this Torch Carrier, for example." Carter tapped the papers in his lap. "Do you recall his letters?"

"Torch Carrier?" Emmy nodded. "Of course. He's been writing me about his college sweetheart, whom he calls 'Susie.'"

"Right." Carter's smile was back in place as he crossed his legs and adopted a cocky posture. "Here's a jerk who has to ask a stranger for advice about putting the moves on an eligible woman. I mean, this guy is so green that, if you planted him, he'd grow!" Carter chuckled and ran a finger over his mustache. "You've taken him through a courtship with Susie, step by step, and this guy is presumably in his late twenties or early thirties! He should know how to score by now! Don't you suspect that his porch light is on, but no one is home?" Carter laughed and glanced at the camera which represented his audience, to share his little joke with them.

Whit's hands balled into fists at his sides, and he wished he could break up Carter's party and punch out *his* porch light. He looked at Emmy and could see her anger mounting into rage.

"T.C. is not a jerk!" Emmy took a deep breath, and her eyes shot blue fire at Carter. "He is a caring man who is secure enough to ask a woman for advice on wooing another woman. Believe me, Mr. Carter, if more men would listen to women about romance, the world would be a lot better off!"

"Yes, but—"

"I'm not finished." Emmy glared at him until Carter shrugged and relinquished the floor. "Most men are great in the sex department, but they could use a few lessons in romance. At least Torch Carrier is wise enough to know that and to accept it. I admire him, and I think Susie is one lucky lady."

Whit grinned and flexed his hands. Go get him, honey. Make Carter wish he'd never opened his big mouth.

Carter's smile was indulgent, and his chuckle was downright placating. He looked directly into the camera and shrugged. "I'm sure we all appreciate the sermon, dear. For those who need instructions on how to make time with the opposite sex, Ms. Bakersfield's book is available at your local bookstore. We'll be back with another guest after this commercial message, so stay tuned."

The red light on top of the camera faded, and Carter stood up and looked down at Emmy.

"That's it for your segment. Thanks for stopping by."

Emmy rose to her feet slowly and lowered her gaze to Carter's outstretched hand. "My publicity director warned me that you enjoyed ridiculing people, but I decided to give you the benefit of the doubt." She ignored his hand and looked into his eyes again. "My mistake."

Carter shrugged. "You came off well. It was a good segment for both of us. No hard feelings?"

Emmy's smile was an arctic blast. "No chance of that. I wouldn't waste *any* feelings on you. Good-bye." She turned away from him, stepped off the dais and started in Whit's direction. Her steps faltered when she saw him, and color rose into her cheeks.

"Whit! What are you doing here?"

"Making an emergency call. I heard there might be a hit-and-run victim here." He reached out and seized her elbow, then pulled her with him from the studio, setting a brisk pace that made her break into a stumbling run to keep up with him.

"I'm okay. Hey!" She jerked her elbow from his grasp. "Where's the fire?" She frowned and adjusted her silk blouse on her slim shoulders.

"Come on. Let's get a taxi." Whit tamped down his temper with difficulty. Now that it was over, he was madder than hell at her for ignoring his warnings. "You could have ruined all the work I've done."

"But I didn't."

"That remains to be seen." He strode toward the stairs and made his way to the lobby, where he waited for her at the door. When he spotted her in the stairwell, he stepped outside and hailed a taxi. Whit opened the back door and helped Emmy inside before he settled beside her.

"Royal Sonesta," he said, giving the driver a cursory glance before dropping into a brooding silence. After a while he felt in control, and he shifted in the seat to face her. Her blue eyes were wary, as if she were expecting his dressing-down. "You could have avoided this whole messy business if you'd followed my suggestion and kept away from that man. For an advice columnist you sure as hell have trouble *taking* advice!"

Emmy placed a hand on his sleeve and purred, "What's wrong, Whit? Do you like your women more obedient?"

He scowled at her. "I'd settle for common sense, but I have a feeling that's a little like asking for the moon."

She snatched her hand from his sleeve. "That's a hateful thing to say!"

"I'm in a hateful mood." He crossed his arms and glared at the back of the driver's head.

"Cool off and we'll discuss this at the hotel. In private."

"Fine." Whit averted his face from her and wondered why he was so angry. You're taking this personally, he cautioned himself. He'd never talked with any of his other clients like this, but he wasn't romantically involved with his other clients. True, Emmy had handled herself admirably with Carter, but she shouldn't have been at that studio in the first place. Didn't she understand that he was looking after her best interests? Why was she always fighting him . . . rebelling against him like a wayward teenager?

The taxi coasted to a stop before the hotel, and Whit and Emmy left it and walked silently inside, then headed for Emmy's room. Emmy went straight to the wet bar and fixed two Scotch and waters, handing one of them to him.

"Now, let's discuss this like adults."

Whit shot her a biting glare. "Think you can handle that?" He tossed the liquor to the back of his throat and felt it add fuel to the fire that was almost out of control within him. "It would be a stretch for you, but I'm game."

Emmy swirled the liquid in her glass before she took a sip. "If we keep this up, Whit, one of us is going to say something we'll regret."

Whit finished the drink and set it on the bar. "Emmy, why in the world did you agree to go on that show?"

"For the exposure. That's why we're here."

"We're here for the right kind of exposure," Whit corrected as gently as possible, but his voice still had a cutting edge to it. "You hired me to conduct your publicity, and you're paying me a chunk of money to do it. Now why won't you let me earn that money?"

Emmy took a deep breath. "I didn't hire you; ACTION did."

"A minor point."

"No, it's not." She finished the drink in two long swallows, and the kick of the liquor made her eyes water. "I handled Carter. You said he'd make me look like a fool, but he didn't."

"He came mighty close to it, lady. Mighty close." Whit paced in front of the window, trying to walk off his mounting irritation. "I thought we'd reached an understanding. I thought you'd finally realized that when it comes to publicity I know best."

"I never reached that understanding." Emmy held up one hand to halt his next remark. "I admit that you know more about it, but I'm learning fast. I thought that *you* had finally realized that I'm not the type of woman who dances when a man whistles a tune."

Whit examined her carefully, trying to find a hint of the

woman he had made love to only hours before. "Last night we—"

"Just because I've slept with you, doesn't mean I'm going to obey your every command."

His temper flared, and he ground his teeth together. "Emmy, if you'd just listen to me . . . if you'd have the good sense to follow my—"

"I don't need another man riding on my coattails and telling me what to do!" She blinked as if her outburst had surprised her; then she turned, so that he was glaring at her back.

"Riding on your coattails?" Whit repeated the part of her tirade that had cut him to the quick. "Is that what you think I'm doing?"

He closed the distance between them, grabbed her shoulders and whirled her around to face him. Her eyes were enormous, shimmering blue pools in a face that had gone pale.

"If that's how you feel, I'll submit my resignation when we get back to Atlanta." He waited, hoping against hope that she would take back what she'd said. When she didn't, he released her and started for the door.

"If you want to handle this by yourself, do it! I don't give a damn one way or the other." He threw open the door and looked over his shoulder at her.

She was still standing where he'd left her, staring at him as if she were hypnotized.

"One more bit of advice before I remove myself from the payroll," he said, wishing he could give her a good shaking and break the self-induced trance she was in. "Even though your advice isn't all it's cracked up to be, it wouldn't hurt if you'd try to follow it yourself!" He slammed the door, closing himself off from the one woman who meant the world to him.

Emmy jerked violently and stumbled toward the door, but her courage deserted her before she could fling it open and beg Whit to forgive her.

She dissolved into a chair and felt tears burn the backs of her eyes. She had known it would end like this. Hadn't she warned him? Hadn't she told him that one of them would say something they would regret? Regrets rained down on her until she buried her face in her hands and surrendered to the tears.

Maybe it was for the best. Maybe she wasn't cut out for this kind of relationship. She hadn't been able to handle it with Jerry. She'd always resented it when he'd given her orders and tried to conduct her business affairs. But she had hoped it would be different with Whit, because he was different.

Oh, why couldn't he understand her reluctance to let go of the reins? He seemed to understand so much about her. Why couldn't he understand this? She leaned back in the chair and stared gloomily at the ceiling as she went over the heated conversation again. Would he really resign? Could she talk him out of it? *Should* she talk him out of it? If he did resign, would he see her on a strictly personal basis?

She closed her eyes and moaned as the answer came swiftly and with the cutting edge of a knife. No, he wouldn't. His pride was at stake here. He'd give up a lot, but he wouldn't give that up. Not even for her.

9

Dear T.C.,

I'm sorry to hear that my advice hasn't panned out for you, but I can't say that I'm completely surprised.

Lately I've learned that my instincts aren't always the best, so try yours. You know Susie better than I do, and you sound as if you're a level-headed, sincere man, so why not let yourself go and just do what comes naturally? Since my previous suggestions have failed you, perhaps you should fall back on a tried but true formula.

Follow your heart, dear T.C., and maybe it will lead you straight into Susie's arms. I'm rooting for you and, judging from the mail I've received recently, so are many others. Best of luck.

Maudie

Whit tossed the newspaper into the trash can, smiled, and began whistling a bouncy tune as he lathered the lower half of his face and continued his morning ritual. Ever since Emmy's first column had appeared in syndication, Whit had begun his day by reading the letters and her answers. It had become a habit which had become more important to him over the past few months. He reached into the medicine cabinet for his shaving utensils, indulging in another habit he had practiced since his father had taught him to shave on his fourteenth birthday.

When Whit traveled, he used an electric shaver, but when he was home he enjoyed taking his time as his father had taught him. He swished the shaving brush around in the old-fashioned mug, then applied another swipe of lather under his chin and down his throat before reaching for the double-edged safety razor.

It was so good to be home again, he thought as he drew the razor down the side of his face. Esmerelda weaved between his legs, and Whit paused in his task to glance down at her. Was it his imagination, or did she look different now that she was a mother? Wasn't there a more mature sheen in her cool green eyes?

"Morning, Elda. Taking a break from your kids?" Whit laughed when the tortoiseshell calico meowed plaintively. "Stop your bellyaching. Now you're paying for your indiscretions."

Esmerelda padded regally toward the bedroom, her tail standing straight up like a royal plume. Whit chuckled and resumed his shaving routine. Pete had kept Elda and her family while Whit had been out of town and, much to

Whit's surprise, Pete had decided that he wanted the kitten who was the spitting image of Elda.

"I never imagined that *you'd* want one of them," Whit had said in disbelief when Pete had inquired about the kitten.

"Bitsy likes me," Pete had said with a shrug as his face turned a bright pink.

"Bitsy?" Whit had repeated with a smirk that had deepened Pete's coloring to blazing crimson.

"Well, she's just a little bitty thing," Pete had murmured, staring at the toes of his shoes. "Anyway, can I have her or not?"

"Sure, pal." Whit had cuffed Pete boyishly. "As soon as . . . Bitsy is old enough to leave her mother, she's all yours."

Pete's smile had held a mixture of relief and pride. "Thanks, Whit! I'll take good care of her. I promise."

Whit dipped the razor into the sink and rinsed it off as he mentally ticked off the kittens. One to go, he thought, then shook his head. No, he'd keep the black one. Why had he made fun of Pete? He was just as silly about the black kitten as Pete was about Bitsy. Although he hadn't spoken the name aloud, he had mentally named the little creature.

"Domino," Whit whispered, liking the sound of it. "Domino and Esmerelda." He laughed softly. All the kittens had been named. Bertha had named hers Brown Sugar. "Brown Sugar, Domino, Bitsy and Prince Charming."

Whit sighed as the thought of Prince Charming focused his musings on the kitten's owner-to-be. Emmy had an uncanny talent for turning him inside-out. The question of his resignation had hovered over them since that afternoon in New Orleans, but neither had touched the subject again. Did she think he had forgotten it or decided not to force the issue? Well, if that was the case, she'd better think again. He was a man of his word and didn't make idle threats.

After wiping the last of the lather from his face, Whit cleaned the sink and replaced the mug, brush and razor in the medicine cabinet. He splashed on cologne, checked his handiwork in the mirror and strode from the bathroom to the telephone beside his bed. He dialed Emmy's home number and smiled when she answered.

"Emmy, it's Whit."

"Whit!" There was a pause, as if she were gathering her self-control and, when she spoke again, her voice was less enthusiastic. "Good morning. I was just leaving for the office."

"I won't keep you. I'm calling about my resignation."

"Whit, let's not fly off the handle." There was a note of desperation in her voice.

"I'd like to submit it in person," he persevered, refusing to be led into a compromising position.

"That's not necessary. In fact, I—"

"Are you free for lunch?" Whit interrupted, steeling himself to the husky sexiness in her voice. "We can discuss the matter then."

"Well . . . yes, that's fine. Can I meet you at one?"

"Yes. How about that place near your office?" He couldn't remember the name of it, but he remembered the last time he'd been there. He had met Emmy there to discuss the publicity tour, and she had given him the first hint at the source of her hostility toward him. She had thought of him as Jerry's friend instead of hers.

"You mean the 'Best Kept Secret'?"

Whit blinked in confusion. "Pardon me?"

"That's the name of the restaurant. The 'Best Kept Secret.' That's the one you mean, isn't it? It's just a few blocks from my office."

"Yes, that's it." Whit smiled at the irony of it all. "I'll see you there at one. Good-bye."

"'Bye, Whit."

Whit replaced the receiver, shaking his head slowly. How appropriate that it had begun in that restaurant, he thought. It was one of life's little ironies, a joke played on him, one that had a cruel twist. His love for Emmy was his best kept secret, but it was time to confess. It was time to come out of hiding and quit playing games. He'd thought that he had a foolproof plan in winning her love, but he'd been wrong. He had nothing to lose now. Nothing to lose, that was, except Emmy.

He was sitting at the same table as before, and Emmy couldn't help but recall the last time she had met Whit in this restaurant. A party of four stood in front of her and waited for their reserved table, and Emmy let them conceal her for a few moments while she feasted on the sight of Whit in his three-piece navy blue suit, paler blue shirt and striped tie. The afternoon sun created a halo around his head, picking out the sandy brown strands in his hair. He sipped thoughtfully on a drink and seemed to be lost in his own world, oblivious to the chattering and bursts of laughter around him.

His long fingers slipped along the sides of the frosted glass, and Emmy vividly recalled the touch of those fingers on her feverish skin. She trembled and ducked back when Whit glanced toward the entrance. Spotting a mirror near the reservation desk, Emmy paused to check her appearance. She wanted to make it as difficult as possible for him to cut her out of his life, so she had chosen her most attractive outfit. Her blue silk jacquard blouse had soft pleats at the shoulders and a stand-up collar. The blouse was tucked into the waistband of a slim, pleated skirt of the same color, and she wore a leather and snakeskin belt of golden brown that matched her low heels and clutch purse.

The skirt and blouse were the same shade as her eyes, eyes that were enormous behind her oval-shaped glasses. She reached up and touched her black hair, which she had gathered into a French twist, then moistened her lips before turning around and sidestepping the group in front of her. Catching the hostess's attention, Emmy nodded in Whit's direction.

"I'm with Mr. Hayes."

"Oh, yes. Please follow me." The hostess set off in Whit's direction, with Emmy right behind her. "Mr. Hayes, your guest has arrived."

Whit stood up and helped Emmy into the chair across from him. "Thank you," he said to the hostess, then looked at Emmy. "What will you have to drink?"

"Bloody Mary, please," Emmy told the hostess.

"Okay, and here are your menus." The hostess handed them the oversized menus before leaving.

Emmy glanced at the menu, recalling the last time she'd been here with Whit and he had teased her when she had squinted at the listings instead of using her reading glasses. The words were clear today, but she had no appetite. Her stomach was churning, a victim of the uncertainty and melancholy she was feeling. A waiter set Emmy's drink on the table and stayed to take their orders.

"Tuna salad sandwich and tomato soup," Whit said, handing the menu to the waiter. "Emmy?"

Emmy shrugged, handing over her menu. "The fruit

plate." She glanced at Whit and offered an apologetic smile. "I had a big breakfast," she lied, preferring not to tell him how his phone call that morning had made her queasy. He wasn't really going to resign, was he? She studied his face and felt a sinking sensation in her stomach. His jaw was tensed, and his eyes held none of the mischievous light she had come to love. He was serious. She stiffened when he reached into his breast pocket and withdrew a white envelope.

"Here it is." He placed it on the table and slid it toward her. "My resignation."

Emmy seized the Bloody Mary and took a long drink of it. "I don't want it," she said, her voice little more than a whisper. She pushed the envelope back across the table to him. "I can't accept it."

Whit lifted his wide shoulders in a careless shrug. "You have to."

"No." She cleared her throat, striving for a stronger tone. "I didn't hire you, so I can't accept your resignation."

"Okay." He tucked the envelope back into his breast pocket. "In that case, I'll submit it to Tom Griven at ACTION."

Oooo, he was so stubborn! Emmy thought, examining his stern expression. Well, she could be just as bullheaded! It couldn't end like this. She removed her glasses and tucked them into her purse, then folded her hands and tried to appear composed.

"Whit, let's not be so hasty. I think you're overreacting. I understand that your feelings are hurt and that I—"

"I'm doing what I think is best—for both of us," Whit interrupted. "You're the one who warned me that mixing business with pleasure was a dangerous combination."

He lifted his Scotch and water in a salute. "You were right."

"Not entirely," Emmy corrected. "I didn't take into account that you're different from—" She cut off her sentence as the waiter approached their table and set their lunches before them.

"You didn't take into account what?" Whit asked after taking a bite of his tuna sandwich and peppering his tomato soup.

Emmy stared at the plate of sliced peaches, pears, tomatoes and watermelon, and felt her stomach lurch. "That you're not Jerry."

"Oh, have you finally realized that?" Whit touched a white linen napkin to one corner of his mouth. "Emmy, I don't want to ride on your coattails or manage your life. I just want to do my job."

"I know." Emmy felt her shoulders slump. This wasn't easy, she thought. It was hard to wrap a man like Whittier Hayes around her finger, if not downright impossible. "I want you to do your job, too. I don't want you to resign."

"I think you've judged me by what Jerry has done to you, and that isn't fair."

"I know." Emmy felt like a broken record, but what else could she say? He was right. She glanced up and realized that Whit was waiting for something more from her. With a little sigh, she pushed aside her lunch and met his expectant gaze. "I promised myself that I wouldn't bore my friends with the unpleasant details of my marriage and divorce, but I guess I should break that promise in this instance."

"I won't hold it against you. I'd like to know what I've been up against."

"I *have* allowed my past experiences to discolor my present relationship with you," Emmy admitted, her fingers plucking nervously at the red tablecloth. "When Jerry struck out in his own career, he decided to manage mine." She glanced up to find that Whit was examining her with an unnerving intensity. "I use the word *manage* very loosely."

Whit smiled, but made no comment.

"I went along with it because I knew that he needed to feel important. Jerry was never a happy person after college, and I gave a lot over to him while we were married, even though I knew he didn't have the business savvy he thought he had." Emmy frowned as the memories poured over her in a drenching wave. "Things rocked along and got out of control. Jerry made some unwise business decisions, and I stepped in and unraveled the mess he'd gotten me into. That's when things went from bad to worse."

She paused to take another sip of her drink before she continued. "During the divorce hearing Jerry's lawyer insisted that Jerry had been my business manager and had a vested interest in my income. The judge believed him and instructed me to pay Jerry a settlement for his work as my manager."

"Why didn't you appeal?" Whit asked, pushing aside his own half-finished lunch.

"Because I wanted it to be over. I wanted to get it past me so that I could reconstruct my life." She smiled, but felt the sadness in it. "Here's the kicker. Jerry is the one who has appealed the decision."

"Why? Sounds to me as if he got the better end of the deal."

"He wants half of what I get on the sale of our house. The judge has agreed to hear his appeal, so it's still not over." Emmy sat back in the chair, feeling drained and despondent. "I've been trying to get Jerry out of my life, and that's why I got off on the wrong foot with you. You were linked with Jerry in my mind, and I didn't trust you—at first." Her gaze shifted to meet his; she wanted to make sure he had caught those last two words. "I trust you now, Whit. I really do."

His smile was warm and understanding. "Don't you feel better now that you've got all that out in the open?"

She returned his smile and felt her despondency lift. "Yes, I do. Thanks for listening."

"Now it's my turn to confess." His chest expanded as he drew a deep breath. He adjusted his tie in an uncharacteristic show of nerves.

"You have a confession, too?" Emmy asked, a little perplexed. Was he going to confess that he had never had any real intention of resigning? That would be welcome news.

"Yes, I have a confession." Whit finished his drink and set the glass down solidly. He stared straight into her eyes. "I was never Jerry's friend. I just hung around him to be near you."

The confession rocked her, making her speechless. Emmy felt as if the breath had been knocked out of her as she stared at Whit. She blinked several times, unsure that she had heard him correctly. Was this a joke? Was he teasing her?

"If I felt anything for Jerry, it was envy." Whit turned his head to look out the window, and Emmy could sense his uneasiness. "I've had a colossal crush on you since college." He laughed under his breath, but refused to face her shocked expression. "Not that I've been totally faithful to your memory, but I've never been able to forget you . . . to get you out of my system. It wasn't an accident or a twist of fate that led Tom Griven to hire my firm. I asked Pete to use his friendship with Tom to get him to hire us because I wanted to be near you."

Finally he looked at her from the corner of his eyes, then winced and returned his gaze to the street. "You're looking at me as if I'd just told you I escaped from a mental institution, but I can't say that I blame you."

The waiter placed the check on the table, giving Emmy a few moments to get her thoughts into some semblance of order. Shock had a firm grip on her, refusing to let go, and she could only continue to stare at Whit's impassive profile as he signed the check and presented a credit card. The idea of Whit Hayes having a crush on her since college was so out of character, so tenderly sentimental, that Emmy was hard pressed to accept it.

"Well, aren't you going to say anything?" Whit asked.

"But you spent so much time with Jerry after I married him, and you hardly ever spoke to me," she said, trying to find a weakness in his disclosure.

Whit shrugged. "You were married, Emmy. I'm not the kind of man who would endanger a marriage, no matter how much I wanted to. Jerry never understood how lucky he was to have you, but I think he realizes how special you are now that he's lost you."

He grew silent as the waiter handed him the credit card slip and cleared the table, but he picked up the thread of conversation when they were alone again.

"Emmy, I don't want to lose you, and that's why I'm offering my resignation. Tell you what . . ." He tapped his jacket, where he'd placed the envelope earlier. "I'll hold on to this for a few days to give you time to think this through. You call me when you've made a decision, okay?"

"Yes, okay." Emmy glanced around the restaurant,

suddenly anxious to leave and be alone with her jumbled thoughts. "I should get back to the office."

"Right. Shall I walk you back?"

"No." She grabbed her purse and stood up. "That's okay. Thanks for the lunch."

"Which you didn't touch," Whit reminded her.

Emmy shrugged. "As I said . . ."

"You ate a big breakfast," Whit finished for her. "Give my regards to Bertha."

"I will." She started to say, "Good-bye," but she couldn't get the word past her lips. Emmy turned and left him, but she caught his slight grimace and knew that her exit had been ungracious and hurried. What did he expect after that bombshell? Within the space of a few minutes, he had blown her previous understanding of what they meant to each other to smithereens.

Whit watched her leave. She practically ran from the restaurant, as if someone had yelled, "Fire!" A vision in blue, she seemed to float away from him like a nocturnal dream dissolving in the morning light. He lifted his hand, summoned the waiter, and ordered another Scotch and water. When it arrived, he sipped it slowly and remembered the shock and disbelief he'd glimpsed in Emmy's expression.

She'd looked beautiful today, and he had ached to hold her in his arms and hear her say that she had wanted him back in college, too. He glanced around the restaurant. Could this place symbolize both the beginning and ending of their relationship? After Emmy had time to think about what he said to her, would she decide it was better if they didn't see each other again?

He'd wondered if she had ever suspected his feelings toward her back in college, and now he knew that she had never guessed how much she had meant to him.

One corner of his mouth rose in a self-mocking grin. And he'd thought he'd worn his heart on his sleeve! As it turned out, his feelings for Emmy had been such a closely guarded secret that she'd never even suspected them.

Well, the cat was out of the bag now, Whit thought as he finished his drink and placed a couple of bills on the table. The ball was in her court, and he could do nothing but wait to hear from her. Was she truly blind to *everything*? She was so intelligent that he had been afraid lately that she was adding two and two together and coming up with the magic number. He'd been playing a dangerous game, ready for the moment when he'd be exposed, but maybe he was more clever than he'd thought. Or maybe Emmy was too close to it all to see the trap he had set.

Poor Emmy, Whit thought as he rose to his feet and made his way through the restaurant and outside. She couldn't see the forest for the trees.

Friday night. The night singles kick up their heels and paint the town.

Emmy laughed softly and removed her reading glasses long enough to rub her tired eyes. She slipped the glasses back on and read the column she had just finished. Good enough, she judged as she removed the paper from the typewriter and fed in a blank sheet to begin another column.

Monday she would fly to Knoxville and continue the publicity tour, so this Friday night was devoted to work instead of fun. She sat back in the chair and looked around her apartment's office. One bookshelf held bound copies of her column, each volume representing a year's work. The other shelves contained reference books in philosophy, human behavior, psychology and sexual behavior. Many were well thumbed; others were hardly used.

Her thoughts circled unerringly to Whit, as they had done often since the uncomfortable lunch she had shared with him three days ago. Would he go to Knoxville with her? Did she want him to?

Emmy pushed her hair back from her forehead in a weary gesture. Should she call him and break the ice? Oh, how she missed him! She had grown to cherish her time with him, and it was painful to think that those times might be over.

Dating and courting were more difficult than she had remembered, Emmy realized with a sad smile. She and Jerry hadn't encountered any trouble in the courting department. It had been the marriage that had been difficult.

A bright thread wove through her dark mood. At least the judge had dismissed Jerry's appeal yesterday. Jerry had been livid, but subdued, as if he had understood that the appeal had been his last hurrah, and that now he had to let go of Emmy and the life he had known before.

Emmy had contacted her real estate agent, and the woman had assured her that she could find a buyer for the house. Emmy would be rid of the house soon, a house that represented the final connection to an unpleasant phase in her life. With any luck, Emmy wouldn't have to see or hear from Jerry again.

Her gaze fell on the columns she had cut out during the week, and she gathered them up to paste them in the volume with the rest of the current year's columns. She started flipping through the clippings, recalling the letters and wondering how the people were making out. She knew that one of them—Naughty in New Orleans—

wasn't doing too well, but what of the others? She found herself looking at the first letter she'd received from Torch Carrier a couple of months ago. Wonder what he looks like? Tall, short, dark, fair?

Emmy closed her eyes and let her imagination paint a portrait of the man. Sandy blond hair, dark brown eyes, tall and lithe, with an athlete's gracefulness. He was in his early thirties with an off-center grin and—

Her eyes popped open in alarm. Hold on a minute! She flipped through the pages and located the ensuing letters from Torch Carrier before an inner voice chided her and made her laugh at herself.

Good grief! She was hallucinating. That was it. She'd been thinking of Whit, and now her mind was playing tricks on her. Whit couldn't be Torch Carrier. He was far too level-headed and self-confident to—

She shook her head, recalling his mischievous grin and teasing eyes. He *did* have a streak of deviltry in his makeup. She paged back to the first letter and began reading Torch Carrier's missives with renewed interest, along with her advice to him. Her heart kicked into overdrive, and her fingers trembled as the pieces of a puzzle began to fit neatly together in her mind.

Maudie had told T.C. to send roses, and Whit had sent roses. Maudie had told T.C. to make Susie understand that he was a man she could lean on, and Whit had urged her to lean on him. Maudie had instructed T.C. to throw a party, and Whit had hosted a party for her at his home. Maudie had suggested that T.C. woo Susie with romance, and Whit had been romantic in Miami and New Orleans. The last letter instructed T.C. to follow his heart. . . .

Emmy felt her eyes widen and her heart skip a beat.

Torch Carrier! Whit had admitted that he'd been carrying a torch for her since college. Could it be true? Could Whittier Hayes and Torch Carrier be the same person?

"Oh, I've been such a blind fool!" Emmy moaned, removed her glasses and covered her face with her hands as the import of her realization lent her twenty-twenty hindsight. "That scoundrel! He's been . . . been using *me* to get to *me*." She frowned, confused by her own explanation; then she laughed at the irony of it all. No wonder he thought her advice was worth two cents most of the time! Lately she had begun to think that Susie was an air-head for spurning T.C.'s advances, but her judgment of Susie made her wince now and feel ashamed.

"I *have* been an air-head," she murmured. "Poor Whit. He must feel as if I've sent him on a wild goose chase."

Emmy thumbed through the mail that Bertha had given her earlier at the office and found the most recent letter from T.C. It was typed neatly on cream-colored paper, just as all the rest had been. She read it, read it again more slowly, and smiled. She turned toward the typewriter, and her fingers moved swiftly across the keys as she answered the letter and marked it "urgent," so that it would be printed as soon as possible. Then, as an afterthought, she removed the "urgent" tag.

It doesn't matter when it's printed, Emmy thought with a satisfied smile. She couldn't depend on Maudie. The ball was in Susie's court now.

The batter struck out, and Pete Bitters leaned closer to the television screen.

"Come on, guys!" he begged. "I've got a twenty dollar bet on you, so get with it!" Pete glanced at Whit. "Want another beer?"

Whit looked at the empty can in his hand and shook his head. "I've had enough. What's the score?"

"Four to two. Haven't you been paying attention?"

"No." Whit ran a hand down his face and sighed. "I can't get my mind focused on anything except . . ."

"Emmy Bakersfield," Pete finished for him. "Are you going to resign?"

"I don't know." Whit shot him a glance. "What do you think?"

"I think you're a goner, pal." Pete chuckled and focused his attention on the game again. "That's it! You've got a man on first; now bring him home!"

Whit stood up and paced restlessly around Pete's living room. The apartment was cluttered, just like Pete's office at work. Heaven help the woman who married Pete Bitters, Whit thought. The poor thing would spend most of her time picking up after him. Whit picked up a coffee cup and made a face at the residue in the bottom of it.

"Ever thought of hiring a maid, Pete?"

Pete tore his attention from the televised game long enough to see Whit set the cup back on the table. "You sound like my mother. I'm going to clean the apartment tomorrow."

Whit lifted a stack of old newspapers and magazines from a chair and sat down. "I thought Emmy would call me by now. She's leaving for Knoxville Monday."

"Maybe her silence means that she expects you to fly there with her."

"I told her to call me when she'd made a decision one way or the other."

Pete stuffed potato chips into his mouth and scrutinized Whit. "Why don't you call her? You should see yourself! You look like a lovesick teenager!" Pete laughed and shook a finger at Whit. "You've got it bad, partner. Real bad."

"Don't I know it," Whit agreed. "I guess I'll go home. I'm spoiling the game for you." He started to get up, but Pete motioned for him to stay put.

"Relax, buddy. Let's discuss this situation." He fell back against the couch cushions. "Okay. She's supposed to call you, but she hasn't. Meanwhile, you're tying yourself in knots waiting for some word from her. Is that about it?"

"Yes."

Pete flung out his hands in a helpless gesture. "So why are you playing this waiting game? It's not getting you anywhere. Why don't you go home and call her?"

"You're right." Whit shot up from the chair and fished his car keys from his jeans pocket. "This is stupid. I might as well call her and hear her decision. Hearing whatever she has to say can't be any worse than sitting around and biding my time."

"Right!" Pete punched the air with his fist. "Go get 'em, champ!"

Whit laughed and stuck out one hand. "Thanks for being my friend, Pete. I could use a dozen more just like you."

Pete shook Whit's hand and grinned. "Will you get out of here so I can watch this game?"

"Sorry, Pete. I hope you don't lose your money on it."

"You and me both." Pete gave a wink. "Good luck."

"Thanks." Whit let himself out and hurried to his car. The drive to Flowery Branch seemed to take hours instead of just forty minutes. He rehearsed what he would say to Emmy when he called, revising it over and over again until he was a nervous wreck when he finally steered the car into his driveway. He got out of the Jaguar and paused to breathe in the musky fragrance of the night. Looking up at the heavens, he remembered scenes of Miami and New Orleans, and his heart swelled with sweet emotions.

He looked at the other houses, where the windows glowed with warm light. Families, he thought, wishing he were part of a couple. Marriage used to be something he avoided, but not anymore. Not since Emmy had swept back into his life and made him realize he was half of a whole. Emmy . . . Emmy. He closed his eyes for a moment and indulged in a fleeting fantasy of Emmy standing in the doorway of his house and greeting him with a tender kiss. He smiled, enjoying the sense of belonging. Oh, she'd be so nice to come home to.

The image dissolved, leaving Whit alone and anxious. He crossed his lawn and bounded up the steps to the porch as he selected his house key from the others on his key ring. As he inserted the key in the lock he heard the phone ringing inside, and he pushed open the door and ran across the dark living room to answer it.

He snatched up the receiver. "Hello?"

"Hello, Whit."

Relief made him limp. "Emmy!" He swallowed, hearing the throbbing hope in his voice. "I just came in. I've been over at Pete's watching the baseball game on TV."

"I'm glad I caught you."

He tried to read something in her tone, but couldn't. "What's up?"

"Oh, I was just finishing up some work, and I remembered that I'm supposed to fly to Knoxville Monday."

"That's right." Whit held his breath and waited for the other shoe to drop.

"Whit?"

"Yes?" His nerves stretched to the breaking point.

"Could you come over tomorrow night for dinner? I think we need to talk, and I'd rather do it face-to-face."

"Dinner tomorrow night?" Whit pushed Esmerelda aside with his foot when she insisted on rubbing against his leg. The cat glared at him through the darkness, then ran toward the laundry room, where her family was crying for a late night snack. "What time?"

"Seven. Is that okay?"

"Yes, that's fine. What can I bring?"

"Nothing. This is my treat."

"Okay. I'll be there."

"Good. See you then."

Whit replaced the receiver and switched on a table lamp. Dinner at Emmy's. Was that a good sign or a bad one? he wondered. Well, at least she had called him.

Dropping into a chair, he went over the possibilities in his mind. The best he could hope for was that this wouldn't be a farewell dinner. A last supper, so to speak.

Esmerelda entered the room and tried again. She leaned against his leg and purred, casting her soulful gaze up to him.

"You're such a shameless hussy, Elda," Whit said, then laughed when the cat jumped into his lap and pushed her head under his hand. "There, there," he crooned as he stroked her sleek head. "Had a bad day, old girl? Are the kids driving you up a wall?"

A thought struck him out of the blue, and he grinned. He stood up, sending Esmerelda to the carpeted floor, and went to his study. Rolling a sheet of paper in the typewriter, he began to compose a surprise document of ownership for Emmy. It was high time to make her the legal owner of that kitten she had grown so fond of. Maybe this would get them off to a good start tomorrow night. Maybe it would pave his way into her good graces again. Who knew? It might be his ticket to Knoxville.

10

Dear Maudie,

I don't want to leave you with the impression that
your advice has been all bad because it hasn't. You've
given me the courage to be honest with Susie and,
should this grand affair not work out, I won't regret
having tried. I'm going to follow my heart. If Susie
returns my love, you will definitely be on the guest list
for our wedding. Sign me your faithful fan,

Torch Carrier

Dear T.C.,

Thanks for the kind words. Susie is a lucky lady, and
I'm sure she knows it by now. As for that wedding you
mentioned, I wouldn't miss it for the world!

Maudie

Juggling the phone between her shoulder and ear, Emmy interrupted Bertha's recital.

"I know what it says, Bert. I wrote the answer. Remember?"

"Yes, but you didn't tag it 'urgent' so that it will be printed as soon as possible!" Bertha's voice rose to near-hysteria.

"I don't think it's necessary. I think T.C. has the matter under control."

"What makes you think that?"

"It's a gut feeling." Emmy smiled at her reflection in her dresser mirror. "Why are you working, anyway? This is Saturday."

"I know, but I was looking through the stuff I picked up from you this morning, and I found this one, and I thought that . . . Are you sure about this? Poor T.C. is probably going out of his mind over—"

"Bertha, trust me on this. He wasn't asking for advice in his last letter. He was signing off. I'd love to debate this with you, but I'm in a rush. If you want to mark it 'urgent,' then go ahead. It doesn't really make any difference."

"What's gotten into you?" Bertha sighed heavily. "Well, okay. I'll let you go."

"Thanks. Good night, Bert."

"'Night, Emmy."

Emmy replaced the receiver and adjusted the shoulders of her taupe wrinkled silk shirt, then tucked it more securely into the matching trousers that bloused at her hips and tapered to her ankles. She clipped on topaz earrings, and fastened a topaz and pearl choker around her neck, then stepped back and admired her reflection as she brushed her shoulder-length hair until it gleamed like strands of silken onyx.

She rolled up the sleeves of the shirt to her elbows and went over the agenda again. Dinner, drinks and a heart-to-heart talk about how much Whit meant to her and how desperate she was to keep him in her life. Most importantly, she wanted to assure him that she believed she could handle a business/personal relationship. He had taught her things about herself, and she had been an avid student. All she asked was that he be more considerate of her desire to be consulted before any business decisions were made, especially now that he knew why she was overly sensitive when a man tried to boss her.

That wasn't too much to ask, was it? Surely not from a man with Whit's compassion and understanding.

This would be an evening they would both remember. Emmy smiled at her reflection and mouthed, *"Lagniappe."* Yes, she would give Whit a big dose of that!

She sprayed her favorite perfume along the insides of her wrists and elbows, and behind her ears, just as the doorbell announced Whit's arrival. Emmy glanced at the clock. Right on time. It was seven o'clock sharp.

Hurrying from the bedroom, Emmy crossed the living room and flung open the door. A bouquet of white carnations, greenery and baby's breath filled her field of vision before she looked past it and saw Whit's twinkling brown eyes.

"Your favorite, right?"

"Right," Emmy said with a laugh as she took the bouquet from him. "Thank you. Come on in." She kissed his cheek and stepped back to let him enter her apartment.

"Mmmm, you smell good." Whit sniffed the air close to her. "Am I early?"

"No, you're right on the button. I'll put these in a vase while you pour us a drink. Make mine white wine." She motioned toward the portable bar in one corner of the room, then went into the kitchen for her most treasured crystal vase. She arranged the flowers in it, placed it in the center of the dining table, which was already set for dinner, and rejoined Whit in the living room.

"Here's your wine." Whit handed her a glass, then extended his own for a toast. "Cheers."

"Oh, you can do better than that," Emmy chided. "Try again."

Whit cast his gaze to the ceiling for a moment in thoughtful contemplation, then touched her glass with his. "Here's to continued success with your book."

"I'll drink to that." Emmy took a sip of the dry wine and smiled. "My editor called today to inform me that my book is heading for the best-seller list. I guess our publicity tour is paying off."

"That, coupled with Maudie's popularity," Whit amended. "Congratulations."

"Thanks." She glanced over her shoulder into the dining room. "Dinner is ready. Are you hungry?"

"Starved. What are we having?" Whit moved with her toward the table.

"Braised beef tips and noodles, plus homemade French bread and a fresh salad with my own special dressing."

"Sounds delicious. By the way, I've brought you a present."

"Something besides the flowers?" Emmy asked, turning toward him.

"Yes." He handed her a brown envelope.

Emmy backed up a step, suddenly wary. Was he handing her that infernal resignation again?

"It's okay," Whit said with a chuckle. "It's not what you think."

Emmy relaxed and took the envelope from him. She withdrew a single sheet of cream-colored paper and laughed softly.

"You're easily amused," Whit noted with drawling sarcasm.

Emmy shook her head. "It's just that I recog—" She cut off the rest of the sentence and unfolded the sheet of paper. "Never mind." She read the words typed in capitals across the top of the page and laughed again. "Ownership papers?"

"This makes it official," Whit explained. "In a couple of weeks you will be the proud owner of Prince Charming."

Emmy clutched the paper to her chest and laughed. "How's that little ball of fur doing?"

"His eyes are open, and he has a fixation with Esmerelda's tail. She smacked him today when he bit her, and our charming little prince hissed at her."

"I'm glad he's showing some spirit." Emmy folded the paper and replaced it in the envelope. "Could you light the candles while I refill our wineglasses?"

"Sure."

While she topped off the glasses, Emmy watched as Whit picked up the lighter she had left on the table and flicked its trigger. A flame, four inches high, sprang up, and Whit jerked his head back in alarm.

"That's some torch you're carrying," Emmy commented softly.

"I'll say! It almost singed my—" Whit's gaze shifted to her, and his eyes narrowed.

"Singed your what?" Emmy asked with cool innocence.

"My . . . my eyebrows." Whit lit the candles and extinguished the flame. "This needs to be turned down," he murmured, making the necessary adjustment. He tried it again to make sure it was no longer dangerous, then set it back on the table.

"Here, have a seat," Emmy said, pulling back the chair at the head of the table before sitting in the one to its right. Whit assisted her, then sat down. "Let's not be formal. Help yourself."

"Okay," Whit agreed. He tasted the salad and nodded his approval. "This dressing is great. What's in it?"

"It's an old family recipe, and the ingredients are a secret. Some people think it's too sweet."

"No, it's just right."

Emmy relaxed and enjoyed the casual dinner. She soaked in Whit's bountiful compliments, taking extreme pleasure in watching him eat with gusto. He accepted a second helping of the braised beef tips and noodles, and consumed half the loaf of bread.

"You must think I haven't eaten in days," he said, patting his stomach. "That was delicious, Emmy."

"I'm glad you enjoyed it." She pushed back her chair. "Would you care for dessert? I have vanilla ice cream and—"

"No, thanks." Whit shook his head regretfully. "I couldn't eat another bite. Maybe later?"

"Later," Emmy agreed. "Let's go into the living room."

"Can I help you with the dishes?"

"No. I'll pop them into the dishwasher before I go to bed. It's no trouble." She led the way into the living room and turned on the cassette player. A piano concerto floated into the dimly lit room, spilling romance into the air. Emmy turned and let her gaze wander lovingly over

175

Whit, who was sitting on the couch. Having removed his jacket, he was rolling up the sleeves of his white shirt. He glanced up at her as he tugged at the knot of his red tie.

"Did I tell you how lovely you look tonight?"

Emmy shook her head.

"You look lovely." Whit glanced around the living room. "You wanted to talk about my resignation?"

She shook her head again. "No. I wanted to talk about us." She crossed the room and sat beside him on the couch. "You threw me for a loop the other day at lunch when you told me you'd had a crush on me since college."

"I know, but I had to tell you. I was tired of keeping it to myself. I half suspected that you already knew."

"I didn't." Emmy rested her head against the back of the couch and sighed. "It's funny how I can sort out other people's lives, but I can't seem to do much for myself. I guess I was so much in love with Jerry in college that I was blind to other men." She laughed softly and turned her head so she could see him. "Not that I didn't notice you. I always thought you were attractive, but I'm the loyal kind. Once I've pledged my love, I stick to it."

"An admirable trait," Whit whispered, and his eyes seemed to glow with an inner fire.

"When you told me about your crush the other day, I thought you were as drifty as a ten-cent compass."

Whit's gaze sharpened, and his smile disappeared as his lips tensed into a straight line.

"But now that I've had time to think about it, I'm touched," Emmy continued, ignoring Whit's intense scrutiny. "And, I have to admit, that I recall feeling certain things for you in college."

"Oh?" Some of the suspicion left his eyes. "Like what?"

"Like feeling a little thrill when I was close to you. I don't suppose you remember, but one time you were pushing me in a swing and—"

"I remember," Whit cut in.

"You do?"

"Vividly."

Emmy looked away, suddenly embarrassed. "I thought . . . well, I thought you were going to kiss me that day."

"I wanted to."

"Why didn't you?"

"You were engaged to a friend of mine at the time."

"Oh, yes, and you aren't the kind of man who would make time with his friend's intended."

"Maybe I shouldn't have been so noble."

"Maybe you shouldn't have." Emmy felt her insides melt under his sensuous scrutiny. "Maybe if you'd kissed me that day we'd be married now and have a couple of kids."

"And maybe you would have slapped my face and reminded me that you were engaged to another man," Whit countered with a half smile.

Emmy tore her gaze from his and sighed. "Who knows? You're probably right. I was more timid in those days."

"Timid? I don't recall your ever being timid. One of the qualities I've always admired in you is your fiery spirit . . . the way you stand up for what you want."

"I was timid in a way," Emmy argued softly. "I was too timid to admit to myself that I was attracted to you, too afraid of what an admission like that would mean. It wasn't until just a couple of days ago that I finally came to grips with it and realized that you've always been special to me." Her gaze found his again and held it. "I'm a lucky lady, and I know it."

"Oh, Emmy." He brought one of her hands to his lips and kissed her fingers; then his lips stilled and he looked at her as if her last words had suddenly registered. "Emmy?"

"Yes?" She waited, and wondered if he were catching on to her game.

"Emmy . . ." He shook his head and released her hand. "I don't want to resign, but I will if you think it's best."

"Let's dance." She stood up and held out her hands to him, barely keeping her laughter at bay when he cast her an irritated glare. "Can't you dance? I seem to recall that you were quite a hoofer in college. Have you lost your touch?"

He rose from the couch and took her in his arms as he fell into the rhythm of the song. Emmy rested her arms across his wide shoulders and pressed her ear to his chest. His heart was hammering, telling her that he wasn't as unperturbed as he appeared.

"I got some good news yesterday."

"Oh?"

"Jerry's appeal was denied. I can sell the house."

"Good for you." He sounded genuinely pleased.

"Yes. The way has been cleared."

His heart skipped a beat, then resumed its loud drumming.

"I don't think Jerry will bother me anymore."

"For your sake, I hope you're right."

"Whit, have you ever been in love before?"

A few seconds ticked by before he answered. "Before? No."

"Have you ever been close?"

"No."

Emmy fell silent, content to feel his arms around her waist and move as one with him. "Isn't this song romantic?"

"Yes."

"You know, romance can go a long way. In fact, some say that romance is the way to a woman's heart."

He drew away from her and stared down into her eyes. "Maudie has written that before."

"Has she?" Emmy glanced away for a moment, then smiled. "She probably has. It's not original."

"No, it's not."

Emmy laughed and stepped out of his arms. "Why are you looking at me like that?"

"Like what?" he asked, still staring at her through narrowed eyes that gleamed with suspicion.

"Like you're a prosecuting attorney and I'm on the witness stand with a lousy alibi."

Whit ran a hand down his face. "I'm sorry. Can we discuss my resignation now?"

Emmy wagged her forefinger at him. "You have a one-track mind, Whittier Hayes."

"Well, this happens to be important to me." He went over to the couch and collapsed there. "I'd like to get this settled, if you don't mind."

"Okay." Emmy shrugged and sat beside him again. "As far as I'm concerned, it's up to you. I think I've grown enough since I've known you to accept a relationship that's both professional and personal."

"You do?"

"Yes." She faced him, wanting him to see her sincerity. "I was wrong to go on that talk show after you'd advised me against it. I should have listened to you, but I acted without thinking. Whit, I don't mind advice. I just don't like orders."

"I wasn't aware that I'd issued any."

"You didn't, but I wanted to make it clear that I wouldn't take any, in case you got the urge to play drill sergeant."

"Emmy, this is your business, and you've made a success of it. All I want to do is help you with the publicity, because that's where I'm successful."

She nodded, giving him a little smile. "Understood. Whit, if you don't think we can work together, then I'll abide by that. The important thing is that, if I can't have you as a lover, I want to keep you as a friend."

"You'll get no arguments from me on that score because I—" Again his sentence slid into a wall, and suspicion jumped into his eyes.

"There you go again," Emmy warned. "You're giving me that look."

"Sorry." He examined her features carefully before continuing, "Emmy, I don't want to submit my resignation. What do you want me to do?"

Emmy leaned closer until her lips were a mere inch from his. "I want you to follow your heart straight into my arms," she whispered.

Whit jerked backward as if he'd walked into a swarm of bees. He shot up from the couch and glared down into her upturned face. "What's going on here?" he demanded none too gently. "Are you playing a trick on me or what?"

"I could ask you the same question," Emmy countered. "But I won't, because the answer doesn't matter anymore." She paused, and felt her lips part in a smile. "Does it?"

His eyes narrowed to slits. "Emmy, don't play with me. This is serious business and—"

"One final word of advice, okay, Whit?" She didn't wait for his permission, but hurried on. "Why not let yourself go and just do what comes naturally?"

"Why, you little . . ." His lips pressed together for a moment. "How long have you known?"

Emmy shook her head. "It doesn't matter." She stood up and loosened the knot in his tie. "Are you mad at me?"

"Are *you* mad at *me?*"

"I asked you first."

"I asked you last."

Emmy smiled and began unbuttoning his shirt. "No." She glanced up in search of his answer.

"No." He smiled, and his fingers tugged the silk shirt from her waistband. "But I wouldn't blame you if you were a little sore at me."

"Why should I be? Maudie and I are like this." She entwined two fingers, and Whit laughed.

"All in all, Maudie is a wise woman," Whit said, dipping his head so that his lips could brush Emmy's shoulder while he released her shirt buttons.

"Yes, very wise," Emmy agreed. "She knows a good thing when she sees it." She yanked his shirt from his waistband, then pushed it off his shoulders and down his arms as she rained kisses across his breastbone.

"She's loyal, too, and I like that. She really took Dan Carter to task when he poked fun at one of her pen pals." Whit struggled out of his shirt, then removed Emmy's.

"No one can call Torch Carrier a jerk and get away with it," Emmy murmured, flinging her head back so that

181

Whit's mouth could blaze up her throat and settle near her ear. "Dan Carter got just what he deserved."

"Another thing about Maudie—"

Emmy moaned and pulled Whit's mouth around to hers. "Whit, you talk too much."

His lips fastened on hers as he swung her into his arms and carried her to the bedroom. He placed sweet kisses on her mouth before he released her so he could shed the rest of his clothes and let her dispense with her own. Emmy pressed her body to his, winding her arms around his neck and glorying in the movement of flesh against flesh. Her tongue darted into his mouth, seeking and finding the answering stroke of his, while her hands smoothed down the back of his head.

Whit stepped forward, making her step back and fall across the bed. His body covered hers with a warm blanket of masculinity, making Emmy arch upward in a purely feminine response.

"Oh, how I've missed you," she whispered huskily. "How I've wanted you."

"All you had to do was call me and I would have been here in a flash." Whit's fingers combed through her hair, then lifted a shimmering pool of it to his nose. He took a deep breath, as if inhaling the fragrance of the sweetest blossoms.

"I had to be sure," Emmy explained. "I had so much to think through. I didn't want to bring you here under false pretenses. I wanted to be absolutely certain of what I wanted."

"And are you?"

"Oh, yes!" She framed his face in her hands and felt her heart swell with a plethora of tender emotions.

"What *do* you want?"

"You," she answered without hesitation. "You and only you."

"And you are all I've ever wanted." His lips sealed his pledge eloquently, leaving no room for misunderstandings.

Their union was gentle and quiet. Brown eyes gazed longingly into blue ones. Hands and mouths remained motionless as inner feelings ran rampant. Time slowed to a leisurely stroll, allowing passion to burn with a pulsating flame instead of a raging fire. Each precious moment was shared, passed back and forth like a loving cup, and each thought was transmitted through eyes that spoke in a silent, ancient language.

Their union was a tapestry of tightly woven threads. Their souls, spirits, hearts and minds joined, and could not extricate themselves even when their bodies parted, only to join again. They tasted each other with tiny, sipping kisses, and touched each other with soothing, healing fingertips.

The world spun on and on, but for a while they weren't part of it. They existed in a world of their own making. A world of sensuous delights and soft murmurings. A world of two who had become one. A world where the only thing that mattered was the love that flowed between them like a rippling stream that lapped gently at their shores and connected them for all time.

Emmy found heaven in his arms, and Whit found paradise in hers.

The evening surrounded them with a cool swath of midnight, but the bed was an oasis of warmth and security, and Emmy didn't want to leave it.

She turned her cheek into the pillow and drank in the

sight of the man stretched out beside her. She could make out his features, but it wasn't necessary. She had them memorized.

Rolling onto her stomach, she rested one hand on his chest and traced the swirl of soft hair there. He jumped slightly.

"Were you asleep?"

"Just dozing." Whit sat up and braced his back against the headboard. The sheet slipped down, exposing him to her thirsty gaze.

Her hand wandered until her fingers caressed him, making him shiver and still her hand with his own.

"Wait," he whispered, then switched on the bedside lamp. Soft light chased away the night.

"What's wrong?" Emmy sat up, too, suddenly afraid that she had fooled herself into thinking that he was hers, and that nothing could take him from her again.

"Nothing." Whit smoothed her dark hair back from her forehead and dropped a kiss on her lips. "I just want to look at you." His gaze moved from her face to the creamy mounds of her breasts. "You're so beautiful." He leaned forward, and his lips enclosed one of her nipples. His tongue darted across it before he sat up straight again.

"Don't tease me unless you mean it," Emmy cautioned, snuggling closer and draping an arm across his waist. "Are you sure nothing's wrong? You aren't having second thoughts, are you?" She looked up into his face, but his expression was taciturn. "Whit? Whittier, answer me!"

He laughed and hugged her to him. "Shhh. You think too much. It gets you into a lot of trouble."

"I wouldn't think too much if you'd talk to me," Emmy complained, holding him fiercely to her.

"But earlier you said that I talked *too much*," he reminded her with a grin.

"Whit," Emmy begged, "don't tease me. Not now. *I'm* not having second thoughts." She drew away from him again and cast him a worried glance. "Are you?"

Whit's chest lifted with a labored sigh. "Let me put it this way . . ."

Emmy waited until she was ready to scream with impatience; then his deep voice floated to her.

"Dear Maudie," he began, ignoring Emmy's startled gaze. "I love Susie beyond belief. I love her so much that it frightens me. No, that's wrong. What really frightens me is the possibility that she will reject my love. Just between you and me, Maudie, I'm tired of carrying this damned torch. I'd like nothing better than to put it down. In your opinion, is there any hope that Susie will return my love? Is there a chance that she loves me, too, and that she's just as frightened that *I* might reject *her?* I'm waiting impatiently for your answer, so please hurry with it. Signed, Torch Carrier."

Emmy smiled and felt her earlier misgivings dissolve. She moved until her breasts were flattened against his chest and she could look into his eyes.

"Dear T.C.," she whispered. "There is always hope where there is love. In my opinion, Susie would have to be crazy to reject the love you offer her, and I think she's a pretty smart lady. I'd wager that the next time you kiss her those bells you hear will be wedding bells. Signed, Maudie."

The corners of Whit's eyes crinkled up as he delivered one of his lopsided grins. His fingers drove through her hair and pulled her head toward him so that his lips could brush hers before settling more firmly.

Passion billowed through Emmy as she returned his

kiss and his love. She felt his desire stir to life before he ended the kiss and drew in a deep breath.

"Can I put down the torch?"

"Be my guest," Emmy replied with a little laugh.

"Ah!" Whit issued a long sigh of relief as his lower body rubbed against hers. "That feels much, much better!"

Emmy laughed and kissed him again. "I just bet it does."

His smile waned, and he met her gaze. "Are you sure you're not mad at me for using Maudie to get to you?"

"On the contrary," Emmy said, pausing for a moment to kiss his cheek, rough with tomorrow's beard. "I admire your tenacity and ingenuity. I just wish I'd followed my own good advice and avoided so many problems."

"Oh, well, it was worth it." Whit grinned and kissed the tip of her nose. "It worked, and that's all that's important."

"Is it?" Emmy asked, finding the answer in the depths of his appreciative eyes.

"It is." His mouth moved lazily over hers, rekindling her passion and his own.

"Dearest Emmy," he said, pulling back a little to see her face. "Will you marry me and make me the happiest man alive? Signed, Your One and Only, Whit."

Emmy swallowed a lump that had formed in her throat and blinked back tears of joy. "Dearest Whit," she answered in a throaty whisper. "How does it feel to be the happiest man alive? Signed, Forever Yours, Emmy."

The Silhouette Cameo Tote Bag Now available for just $6.99

Handsomely designed in blue and bright pink, its stylish good looks make the Cameo Tote Bag an attractive accessory. The Cameo Tote Bag is big and roomy (13″ square), with reinforced handles and a snap-shut top. You can buy the Cameo Tote Bag for $6.99, plus $1.50 for postage and handling.

Send your name and address with check or money order for $6.99 (plus $1.50 postage and handling), a total of $8.49 to:

Silhouette Books
120 Brighton Road
P.O. Box 5084
Clifton, NJ 07015-5084
ATTN: Tote Bag

SIL–T–1

The Silhouette Cameo Tote Bag can be purchased pre-paid only. No charges will be accepted. Please allow 4 to 6 weeks for delivery.

Arizona and N.Y. State Residents Please Add Sales Tax

Offer not available in Canada.

READERS' COMMENTS ON SILHOUETTE DESIRES

"Thank you for Silhouette Desires. They are the best thing that has happened to the bookshelves in a long time."

—V.W.*, Knoxville, TN

"Silhouette Desires—wonderful, fantastic—the best romance around."

—H.T.*, Margate, N.J.

"As a writer as well as a reader of romantic fiction, I found DESIREs most refreshingly realistic—and definitely as magical as the love captured on their pages."

—C.M.*, Silver Lake, N.Y.

"I just wanted to let you know how very much I enjoy your Silhouette Desire books. I read other romances, and I must say your books rate up at the top of the list."

—C.N.*, Anaheim, CA

"Desires are number one. I especially enjoy the endings because they just don't leave you with a kiss or embrace; they finish the story. Thank you for giving me such reading pleasure."

—M.S.*, Sandford, FL

*names available on request